I0763544

WING MAGIC

Other Series by Sarah K. L. Wilson

Dragon School

Dragon Chameleon

Dragon Tide

Bridge of Legends

Tangled Fae

Wing Magic

Empire of War & Wings
Book 3

Sarah K. L. Wilson

Published by Sarah K. L. Wilson, 2020

This is a work of fiction. Similarities to real people, places, or events are entirely coincidental.
HIVE MAGIC
First Edition. October13, 2020

ISBN : 978-1-7772645-2-9
Cover Art by Luciano Fleitas
Written by Sarah K. L. Wilson
www.sarahklwilson.com

For Cale, always.

N
W
E
S

FORBIDDING TAKEN LANDS
FAR REACH
VLAREN
KARKATUA
FAR STONES
A COLONY OF THE WINGED EMPIRE

ELSEWHERE IN THE WINGED EMPIRE

Wing Etruna sat cross-legged in the crow's nest, breathing in the scent of the sea while her blue jay dove and soared around her. In a moment, the gong would sound, and she'd need to climb down to receive orders for the week. In a moment, this glorious freedom she felt from so high in the air would disappear and she'd crash back to reality but for now, it was only her and Izusa and with her eyes closed she could see through the eyes of her spirit bird as he soared and wheeled over the Imperial Tern Fleet. She liked to believe that when this life was over and the skies received her, that she could be a bird with him soaring through eternity side by side.

Her bliss was interrupted as her jay spiraled in closer over the Fleet. Something was happening. Something big. Runners raced down the docks and where they found ships' captains, orders were barked and men and birds leapt into action.

Someone shook her shoulder and her eyes flew open, breaking the connection with her bird.

"Wing Etruna!" the ship's boy shook her again. "The Captain needs you. Now. By order of Le Majest, we sail."

"The Flycatcher sails?" Wing Etruna gasped, still shocked by her sudden return to her own flightless body.

"We all sail. The whole fleet," the boy said, practically dancing with excitement. "We go to quell our enemies in the Far Stones!"

BOOK ONE: FLIGHT OF THE BEE

The hum in your chest,

The song in your heart,

The cry from the heights,

Echoes in every part.

We're none of us meant,

For kissing the dust,

In hope, we will rise,

And do what we must.

Songs of the Winged Ones

CHAPTER ONE

My mouth was dry and thick. I tried to swallow. Even that hurt as I pulled my limbs under me to sit up. There had to be water somewhere. Something pressed on me in the darkness.

"Don't move." Zayana's voice was barely a whisper. "Stay still."

I froze at the urgency in her tone and tried to listen.

Around us, voices called to one another. My eyes began to adjust to the darkness, and I realized I was under a covering in the front of a boat. I could hear the water lapping against the hull and smell brine. We were in the sea, then. This boat was too small for that. It rocked back and forth, yawing precariously. My belly rolled in response.

Oars banged against the hull and the muffled sound of voices again broke through the cloth covering me. I moaned without meaning to and a bee slipped from my hand, manifesting and hovering in the close air under the tarp. Warmth flooded me and with it, a gasp of reassurance as the bee lit the tiny space I was in.

How long had I been passed out and lying here? My whole body ached, my injuries flaring hot and angry.

I opened the edge of the cuff around my wrist to look at Os's feather. It glowed purplish-white but when I touched it, it was only warm, not hot like it would be if Os was near. I breathed a sigh of relief and closed the cuff. Wherever we were, we had not yet been caught. Something had delayed Osprey. Perhaps he was too injured to pursue us.

The light filtering through the tarp went dark suddenly and the sounds above me seemed louder and more echoey than before. The minutes passed slowly as my throat grew drier and my thirst greater. After my bold words and actions just hours ago, it seemed wrong to be hiding under a tarp in a boat like a smuggler.

I couldn't have said if it was hours or just very, very long minutes until finally the tarp was dragged back and Zayana silently offered me a waterskin.

I drank from it thirstily, grateful to lean into the refreshment of water. When I was done, I met Zayana's worried eyes.

"Thank you," I whispered.

She nodded tightly, looking around us with big eyes.

We were in our boat, but this section of water was surrounded by close wooden slats which formed a room barely bigger than the boat. A ladder climbed up from the center of the small room through a trap door above. I could just barely make out the sound of Ivo's voice through the trap door. He was speaking to someone quieter than he was, and I couldn't hear them at all, only the cadence of my Guide's voice as he replied to the quieter speaker.

"It's almost noon," Zayana whispered. "We fled down the coast through the sea to this place. Wing Ivo knows someone here."

Her hands were clenched in her dress and there was no sign of her bird.

"Where is Flame?" I asked but she just shook her head. She was so tense I could have used her for a shelf, stacking books or tools on her tight shoulders and fidgeting hands.

"Are you hurt?" I whispered. Fear gnawed at me. Just because Osprey wasn't close didn't mean other Claws were not nearby. Everyone would be watching for us now.

She scoffed, her eyes suddenly wide and glassy.

"No, of course not. My life is just ruined, and the life of my sister, and the hope that either of us might survive the year. Nothing to trouble crazy rebels like you and Wing Osprey."

"What do you mean 'the life of your sister'?" I asked. "She isn't tied to your obedience in some way, is she?"

After all that had happened, I wouldn't be surprised if the Empire had done something like that to her, too. I searched Zayana's pained face, afraid of what I might find there.

She scoffed. "Only in the same way your family is. In the same way all families are. It wasn't supposed to be like this! When Wing Xectare and Wing Ivo fought over who would be my Guide, I saw three gulls and one dove into the water. That's supposed to mean good fortune for the person who sees a change in circumstance! It's not supposed to mean disaster, and yet it was barely an hour later that the city was attacked and now we're fleeing Le Majest and even with all I did for him, I doubt he will remember and be merciful."

Well, she was right there. He certainly would not be merciful. And now he saw me as his own even more than he had before. I fought to keep my breathing measured and even but the slightest slip into remembering that made fear ricochet through me. Loathing and terror were things you could always count on with Juste Montpetit. But it worried me to see Zayana breaking like this. She was usually so careful and cautious. I thought I even saw tracks on her face from drying tears. Had she been crying before she got me that water?

"What am I going to do?" she whispered, covering her face with her hands.

"Join us," I said quietly. "That's what you'll do. It's the best place for you."

"And what? Watch my sister punished in my place?" Was she crying behind those hands? I wasn't good at knowing what to say to help with crying.

"You can't do anything else," I reminded her. I was trying to put myself in her place. Trying to imagine wanting this life and then having it snatched away by the goals of other people – goals I didn't even share. I could see her perspective, but she needed to be practical, too. "You're here with us and you're already branded a traitor, so you might as well join us all the way. You've seen what's happening. You've seen all the injustices. You've seen that snake the crown prince manifested. You've heard the things he said to us. Why not join us and find a different path?"

"You're wrong," she whispered.

I involuntarily drew backward. Wrong? Was she crazy? She'd seen what I saw! How could she think the Winged Empire was still something to follow or engage in? Didn't she see that my hands were shaking just from the memories?

"I do have options," she continued. "I could just find the nearest Claw and turn you in."

I swallowed. I hadn't expected that.

She pulled her hands from her tear-streaked face so suddenly that I worried for her.

"Sign," she gasped, "I need a sign."

"O … kay," I said. She was in worse shape than me, despite the pain I was in from the beating last night. My eye throbbed and my belly hurt so much that I wasn't sure I could stand up straight. But I couldn't' think about me right now. I needed to slow down and help Zayana. "Where do you learn about these signs? There sure are a lot."

"My nurse taught me," she said with a look that suggested I'd asked her how she'd learned to dress herself. "Just like all children on the mainland are taught."

"Well, you seem to believe it more than the others I've met."

"I have faith." She said that with a trembling lip like her faith was on the edge right now. She was studying the wood around us, looking for her sign.

"Maybe you could send Flame to go and look after your sister," I suggested. After all, I had sent my bee. It brought me a lot of comfort.

She rolled her eyes. "He'd fade in a mile. A useless plan."

"How do you know?" I pressed. After all, my bees did not fade in a mile. Even now, I was picking up little flashes from them. Ixtap, nursing a gash he'd gotten in the fight. His snake wrapped around it as if trying to caress it better. Someone – Juste, maybe? – huddled in a dark corner sobbing. Wow. He must have liked me even more than he let on with all that marrying business. I'd broken his heart. Or maybe he was even more unhinged than I had feared. I swallowed at the memory of my last minutes with him. If he ever got his hands on me, he would tear me to pieces.

You'll be fast and smart and that won't happen, Aella. I stroked the bracelet Osprey had given me, more grateful than ever for a way to know where he was. But then I shook my head. Every time I thought of him I saw mental images of him descending on us and ripping us to pieces with Os's talons. That was not helpful. Think of something else. Anything else.

"A knothole with a saw cut running through it!" Zayana gasped, pointing at what she'd seen.

"I guess that would be common in any construction project." I looked around at the rough job done on the walls.

Her eyes narrowed.

"But even so," I said, trying to salve her hurt feelings, "you still saw it while you were looking for a sign."

She relaxed, running a hand through her long dark hair. Even now, it was smooth as a sheet.

"It means broken ties," she said, her face twisting like she was going to cry again.

I held my tongue. Maybe she would just decide to join us if I let her interpret her signs. After all, 'broken ties' had to mean her ties to the Winged Empire.

She gasped.

I waited but eventually, my curiosity got the better of me. "What is it?"

"Two ants caught in a spider's web."

"What does that mean?" And how in the world could you go through life seeing signs in absolutely everything? You'd never get anything done!

"Absolute loyalty. The binding of your heart to another's."

Well, that sounded promising. She could break her ties to the Winged Empire and be a loyal revolutionary. I smiled and very cautiously, she joined me.

"Thank you for sending Flame to rescue me from that awful place." It was easy to sound genuine. "I wouldn't have escaped without him."

She shook her head. "I didn't rescue you. He was just supposed to look for you."

"Well, then I'm doubly blessed," I pressed, but she looked uncomfortable at my gratitude.

I was saved from this quagmire of shifting emotions by Wing Ivo opening the trap door above us and motioning for us to climb. I grabbed the ladder first and pulled myself up, forcing myself to ignore the stabbing pains through my belly where the Claws had kicked me. One day, I'd pay Juste back, blow for blow. I'd take his precious kingdom out from under him and free my people. And I'd escape the clutches of Osprey to do it.

I felt a stab of guilt at that. Because though he would hunt us down and utterly destroy us, he didn't want to. It was hard to fully blame a man for doing a thing he didn't want to do to save the lives of other people. He was probably in more pain than I was after all the times he stabbed himself to try to distract Juste from me. And from that stab to his chest. I shivered at the memory of doing that to him and was grateful when Ivo's weather-worn hand grabbed mine and helped me up into the room above. I needed the distraction. I could hardly bear to think of Osprey right now.

"My friends will lend us horses," Wing Ivo whispered as I looked around the small room. Tables were laid out with buckets and large barrows. The place smelled strongly of fish – both fresh and rotting. I fought against gagging. Ivo gave me a pleased smile and I returned it. "And they'll provide us with supplies, since we are caught without them. Our hunter will expect us to flee into the Forbidding. It would make the most sense, since our skills are strongest in the wilderness, but we will not make this easy for him. We'll flee into civilization, rather than out of it."

My heart sank at the thought. "Won't there be more ways for us to be caught with so many Wings and Claws along the way?"

"We'll just have to be more careful than ever," Wing Ivo said, helping Zayana up the last rung of the ladder into the fisherman's wharf house. "Whatever you do, keep your voices down and your faces out of sight."

"I'm sick of constantly running from something," I said, crossing my arms over my chest. "I want to run to something."

"One thing at a time, girl!" Ivo's voice was a growl as he crept to the door and looked through the slats.

"This general – the one with the two ravens. I want to find him," I insisted. If I was going to keep from going crazy with worry, I needed a goal.

"So did everyone for a few years. And then we all lost hope. Wherever he is, he's passed our reach," Wing Ivo said distractedly. "It's been more than a decade since he was taken. Even if he lives, he is lost to us."

"He lives," I said firmly. My visions of the Hissan had been real.

"Then let him keep living – and let us keep living, too, and for that, we must flee."

"Osprey will catch us eventually," I said, my belly rolling at the nerves that washed over me just from speaking my fears aloud.

"It's amazing that he hasn't caught us already."

Ivo said nothing, but Zayana shifted her weight uncomfortably.

"I want to have accomplished something before I'm dragged off to be married to the crown prince," I said stubbornly.

"Married?" Ivo's head whipped around.

"That's what he said he'd do after he was done torturing me." I couldn't keep the acid out of my voice. "He wants my bees."

"You are the fiancée of Le Majest?" Zayana asked in awe.

I shook my head. "I don't want to be."

"But he said it was so?" she pressed.

I shrugged, refusing to say it aloud. It would feel too real if I admitted it a second time.

"Then you are," she said, her eyes huge. She took a step back as if she was too nervous to be close to someone as honored as me. Juste should have chosen her. She would have given him all the respect and attention he craved.

Ivo's brow furrowed for a long moment, his eyes turning inward and then he nodded slowly. "If we want to find your general, we need to know where to look. I wasn't there when he was taken and rumors are twisty things. Who knows where they have curved into lies? We'll need to go read the records of the battle for Karkatua."

"Does that mean we need to go back to Karkatua?"

"No. The records are kept in the city of Glorious Ingvar in the Oriole Monastery. We'll have to go there."

The door swung open suddenly and a young man hurried in. "Master Alson says to put these on. Hurry."

He handed us dark cloaks – far too warm for the weather. I put mine on anyway, pulling the deep hood up to cover my face.

We followed him out the door to where three horses were being hurriedly saddled. A man in fishing garb looked up, nodded sharply to Ivo, and then returned to his work as he spoke.

"It's all I could spare. Even the horses … well, it's a lot to ask, friend."

"By the time we are finished, there will be more asked," Ivo said grimly. "We will all be asked for our blood – rich and red – and only those who pay in suffering will still stand."

His friend made a sad sound of agreement and then motioned to us to mount. "Be safe. Be fast."

And then he and the young man disappeared into the wharf house and Wing Ivo motioned to us to hurry.

None of the horses looked like they were very high in quality. They were nags meant to pull fish carts, not fine racers, but they were better than nothing. My horse had a paint coat that was rough and shaggy and smelled strongly of fish. She rolled her eyes at the sight of me and I narrowed mine in return.

"Hurry," Ivo reminded. "And try not to be seen."

We mounted quickly and set out, following his shaggy black horse down the docks and skirting the small fishing town beyond. I'd never been to this town – whichever it was – and it seemed I wouldn't be going into it today, either.

Ivo set a punishing pace to the road and once we were on it, he kicked up his horse. There was no talk. No discussion. Just silence.

We could all feel the pressure of the chase and the burden of the hopes of people like that fisherman. Urgency lit the hooves of our horses aflame and we rode fast and hard. And fear pressed down on me, like a leaden weight that would not let up until it drove me into the ground.

I kept feeling for the feather in my wristband, but though I was certain that Osprey was right behind us, it remained still and cool to the touch.

CHAPTER TWO

The hours seemed to pass at a snail's pace as we watched the road and sky with equal worry. The sides of the road showed no sign of the Forbidding, but that didn't make me feel safe. I'd grown too used to seeing trouble there and the fact that there was no tangle of dark magic to hack at only made me feel more and more that there would be one coming soon.

I asked Ivo for my short sword – still strapped to his waist – but he refused me.

"I can wear one since I am a Wing, but anyone else wearing a sword will only draw suspicion. We need to avoid attention at all costs."

And avoid attention, we did, sticking to the road and keeping our eyes down as other travelers passed. Any one of them could report seeing us to Le Majest. Any one of them might already be looking for us. It wasn't long before a trickle of travelers on the road grew to a steady stream and we found ourselves passing hay wains, farmers with goats they were herding to market, carts laden with salted fish, and high-sided wagons that jingled with the sounds of bottles.

Exhaustion ground down on us. I hadn't slept more than a few hours in the past two days, and despite my gnawing anxiety, I could barely keep my eyes open as the steady movement of the horse rocked me. Every bone and muscle in me ached – my injured eye and belly most of all. I kept pulling the hood of my cloak forward, hoping no one would notice my eye.

At one point, a vision rocked me – my bee watching as a healer dressed wounds. Which bee was this? The one I'd left with Juste? But Juste had no wounds to dress and that skin was too dark. It took me a moment to realize it must be Osprey – that these were the stab wounds he'd inflicted on himself in his insanely noble effort to save me from harm. There were so many of them – some deeper than others – and I flinched as salve was applied and torn skin stitched.

I should be grateful for surely this would slow him down – even if he was getting help in a town along the way it would still delay him for long enough to bind these wounds. But I was not grateful for that. With every stitch applied I felt a mirrored pain. He'd done all of that to try to keep me safe.

When the vision vanished, I found my eyes stinging and wet. I dried them hastily, hoping the others wouldn't see.

We reached another town after an hour of traveling out of the fishing village, and another an hour after that. I swallowed at the sight of so many people – dozens on the road and hundreds in some of the towns we passed. Some of them peered curiously toward us and I quickly looked away, keeping my hood pulled low and my face in shadows.

When I accidentally met Zayana's eye, her look of scorn made my face burn hot. So what if I wasn't used to all the people yet? So what if they made me nervous? What special use did so many people have that it was a good thing to be among them?

An army, I decided. They would be good for an army.

After that realization, I watched with different eyes. Instead of looking at the sheer numbers and strange Houses represented, I saw men eyeing the forest just as nervously as I did, feeling at an empty spot on their belts and then clenching their jaws. Instead of women with new hairstyles, I saw how their shoes were worn, the toes almost broken through and no money to replace them. Instead of watching the sheer number of livestock we passed, I noticed how they seemed thin, their eyes spooked as they rolled past.

But I also watched for any hint of betrayal – of any hint that someone was hurrying off too quickly or tying a message to a pigeon's leg. We were prey – and I must never forget that. Hunted, chased, harried. Our only hope now was that we could hide among the harmless people of these towns and escape notice.

When the first Claw division came thundering down the road, mounted on carabaos, I almost missed seeing the looks on the faces of townspeople. I was so busy trying to look normal, trying to still my racing heart and calm my frantic puffs of breath that I almost missed their resentment. Some of it was close to rage as it flickered across every face. Their shoulders were hunched, and eyes turned down, but not out of submission. I saw their knuckles clench white on anything they were holding, their mouths tight with anger.

I didn't dare let my bees loose, but I could feel them within me, furious and buzzing with the anger of the people and the fear in me. They almost seemed to resonate with what was around us instead of just what was inside of me. We all felt the yoke of the Winged Empire settling heavily on our backs. Maybe Ivo was right. Maybe the people were ready to give their very blood to lift that yoke.

We settled for the evening in someone's back pasture just past a small town. Zayana looked longingly at the smoke drifting up from the fires of the inn we'd passed, but Ivo shook his head grimly.

"The town is too small. They'd remember us. This is safer. There's no Forbidding to worry about in this place and we can sleep quietly. Here, eat some bread."

There had been bread stowed in the saddlebags along with a blanket for each of us, skins of water, and not much else. Wing Ivo still had his leather pack, but Zayana and I were starting to feel our poverty. We had no way to clean or tend ourselves, no mirrors, no way to clean our teeth, nothing. Miserable and spent, we sank into our thin blankets. I didn't know if the others felt as hunted as I did, but I looked often at the sky, worried about Osprey's pursuit. I knew him too well to think those wounds would hold him back for very long.

Wing Ivo snorted at us. "Bold revolutionaries one minute and then sniveling girls the next. Stop looking so fearful. We have a little space here and I can help you with your manifestations. When we reach Glorious Ingvar, the city is large enough that we can take rooms at an inn without fear and I will give you coins to shop for what you need, hmm?"

I smiled, trying to pretend I wasn't as worried as I was, and his answering grin made me feel warmer than the blanket.

"Now, call your manifestations, and let's see what we can do with them."

"I just want to sleep," Zayana moaned.

"You can sleep when you've tended your bird," Ivo said firmly. "You need to practice tending, and so does Aella. We're not safe yet and this is more important than sleep."

I opened my palm and a bee popped out almost before I could stop it, buzzing around my head angrily. Five more followed and in moments I was almost swallowed by them.

Ivo made an irritated sound in his throat. "I think I will work with Zayana tonight. Go a little way off, Aella, and try to calm those bees. I can already feel a sting from one of them rising on my neck. You can't tend magic so wild that it strikes at everyone nearby. Think of calm things to say … if you know any."

The wryness of his tone made my cheeks heat. I knew how to be calm! I did. It had just been a while since I felt that way.

I stalked off to the edge of the trees, bringing my thin blanket with me. I found a quiet place and slumped to the ground, wrapped in the blanket. I glanced worriedly back up at the sky. My bees swirled around me, stinging me on my hands and arms.

"Really? You're still doing that?" I complained. But words like that wouldn't help. "I forbid you from stinging me."

That did nothing, either. Quietly – being sure that no one could hear me – I tried a song. It was a song that my father used to sing to me when I was a child. I had always found it calmed me.

My bees grew more agitated, stinging me a half-dozen times in a few seconds. Maybe it was only my poor singing voice, but it felt personal.

Frustrated, I shook them off and tried something else.

"Fine, you want to be mad? Go ahead and be mad!," I told them. "I'm angry. You'd better believe I am. Anger is better than fear. It cripples you less. Think I don't have a good reason to be angry? I'm on the run again, hunted by someone who is supposed to be my friend and when he finds me, he'll drag me off to be the wife of a villain from a Forbidding Tale. Me! I'm not even pretty. It should be someone with long flowing hair and a voice like an angel who can enchant him into sparing her life and all her people, but we all know I'll be the opposite because I'm not a sweet, nice girl. I'm Aella. I'm angry and I'm direct and I just want my freedom and to protect the freedom of the people I love."

Strangely enough, my fury seemed to calm them down to a dull buzz. I swayed against exhaustion. I could just lie here. Just for a moment. I could talk to my bees lying down as easily as sitting up, right?

I lay down on the stony pasture ground, not even caring that the rocks pressed into my ribs. My eyelids flickered and I mumbled to my bees.

"I complain about you, but you are actually a real asset. You were there when I needed you. You caught me when I leapt from the balcony. You were there to free me from Juste. Those are things I'll always be grateful for. And you sent my message to my family. That was very important. And you are my eyes, watching friends and enemies alike."

There was another flicker of a vision after I said that. A vision of someone looking over the city of Karkatua. I saw the buildings, small and rolling out before the person's vision. The sight came and went so quickly that I couldn't see whose perspective I was looking from. Perhaps the crown prince was still surveying the damage from where his allies attacked the people he was supposed to shelter and guard. And no, I wasn't at all bitter about that.

My eyelids were growing heavy. I fought them as I began to mumble.

"If you could just channel all that fear and anger into a cause – like me. If you could use it like you did in the city to protect people and help them see. If you could find my family and guard them. If you could help me escape evil and cling to the good. If you could hold me together with … your … buzz."

I didn't realize I'd fallen asleep until I felt something burning my fingers. I woke with a start.

I'd tucked my fingers into the edge of my wristband without realizing it and the heat of Os's feather had scalded them.

I scrambled to my feet.

My bees were gone. My blanket damp. I stumbled back toward where our camp had been. My feet were both painfully slow and far too loud at the same time. I didn't dare cry out. The rocks were wet. A drizzle of rain was making everything slick. It dampened my hair and face.

Almost there.

Above me, thunder cracked, splitting the air like a hatchet. I jumped. Was it Osprey? Of course not. Just thunder. Powerful though he might be, he didn't create the thunder.

I scrambled into the camp where Ivo sat opposite the fire from Zayana. His voice was a patient drone as he taught her. I couldn't have been asleep for very long, though it was fully dark now and it hadn't been before. And the fire was new.

"Osprey," I gasped, stumbling into camp.

"Where?" Ivo asked, leaping up and drawing his sword free. Would he really fight his friend? My heart lurched at the thought.

"I don't know," I gasped. "He gave me an armband. It tells me when he's near."

Zayana's eyes narrowed suspiciously, but she kicked dirt over the fire with a delicate toe and shook out her blanket.

The thunder cracked again, rippling through the sky and as if it had torn a waterskin, rain descended in sheets, wiping out whatever was left of the fire. A horse whickered nervously, but the rain was so loud that it blocked out all other sound. Ivo was trying to say something, but I couldn't hear him.

He leaned in, grabbed us both by the cloaks, dragging us in close and yelling into our faces.

"The storm may be our salvation." He thrust something into my shaking hand. It felt like my short sword. "Try to stay together. If we are separated, meet me at the Dawn's Forbidding Inn in Glorious Ingvar."

He reached into a pocket and jammed something into Zayana's hand and then something into mine as well. Coins, by the feel of them. I tucked them into my belt pouch and then tried to put my scabbard onto my belt but he shook me.

"No time for that! Mount up!"

He shoved us toward the horses as lightning stabbed down into the pasture, making everything seem to freeze for the split second that it rent the darkness with brilliant light. In the instant of brightness, I thought I saw a silhouette above us.

I scrambled for the horse, narrowly avoiding her stamping feet. She tossed her drenched head, eyes rolling with fear. I untied her from the picket, fitting her bridle on awkwardly. My fingers were clumsy and I'd jammed my sword scabbard into my belt in a way that made it hard to bend. The seconds raced and dragged at the same time as I tried to finish her buckles, fingers slipping as my pulse raced.

Ivo and Zayana were already mounted. They motioned to me

to hurry.

I scrambled up into the saddle, still not sure that the bridle was fitted correctly. I'd just have to hope my horse could follow the others. They were already running before I'd sorted out my stirrups. I could barely see their horses' rumps in the pouring rain.

Lightning streaked down again, followed by the crash of thunder almost instantly. The storm was right over us.

My horse followed the others and I thought we were following the road again, but in the heavy rain, I couldn't tell. We could have been on farmer's fields. And if we were, my horse could break a leg any second in a gopher hole or rut.

I reached into my cuff and singed my fingers. Was it possible that the feather was even hotter? Fear washed my careful approach away and I leaned over my saddle, hunched forward over my horse as she ran. Wind snatched my hood, pulling it off my head and I was instantly drenched, my bushy hair tamed for once by the fury of the storm. I caught a bare glimpse of Zayana's horse ahead of me when lightning shot down, slicing the very air with its fury, and then nothing.

A faint cry came from behind me. It sounded like my name but though I looked behind me, I was too blinded by the rain. The wind snatched at the blanket wrapped loosely around me and it flew away. I thought I saw a blur of light behind me that went out as the blanket swallowed it up.

That was my imagination, that was all. That couldn't have been Os right behind me, could it? I was seeing things.

I turned back to the horses. Forbidding take it!

I'd lost them completely. I sucked in a breath, scanning

frantically through the sheets of rain around me.

A tree branch thwapped me in the face, stinging my cheek. I bit down a curse. Somehow, we'd turned off the road into the forest.

I tried to slow my horse with the reins, but she wouldn't respond. The halter slipped off, falling loose. I pulled it up to me, hand over hand, trying not to lose it entirely. I knew what the problem was. I hadn't snugged the bit tight enough. My horse didn't understand what I was trying to communicate. There was no way to slow her terrified gallop and no way to stop.

I gritted my teeth, held on to the saddle, and ducked my head down to try to avoid the worst of the branches. The short sword dug into my belly, but I didn't dare adjust it. I might need it very soon – to defend myself against Osprey or to put down this poor horse if she broke her legs in holes on the forest floor.

It felt like we ran for hours. When my horse finally slowed, the rain was still pouring down in such heavy sheets that I could see nothing at all. Reluctantly, I dropped from the saddle into ankle-deep streams running across the forest floor.

Her bridle hung in the reins wrapped around the saddle horn where I'd looped it. With a curse, I tried to feel her head and mouth to see if it had been damaged. She bit me – hard.

"Fine," I spat. "Be that way."

I shouldn't be angry at her. She was as frightened as I was and who knew what damage I'd done by not fitting her bridle correctly. I corrected it now, fumbling in the darkness and rain. I was bitten a second time for my trouble.

I shouldn't have leapt on her back until I knew the bit was right. I shouldn't have fallen asleep in the field. This was all my fault. I tried not to sink into self-pity, but tears were close and it was all I could do to hold them back.

When I was done, exhausted and soaked, I led the horse to the bole of a large tree, leaned against it, and fell half-asleep standing up with her reins in my hand. I didn't even care if I was soaked to the skin and holding the reins of a terrified horse. I was too tired to go on. Too tired to care.

I tucked my hand into the leather cuff. Please don't find me, Osprey. It was still warm, but not like it had been.

The thunder and lightning ceased as I blinked in and out of short snatches of sleep. And then, slowly, the rain began to lessen. When dawn finally crept into the world, l shook myself to alertness.

I was in the middle of a forest of large trees. Large enough, fortunately, that the brush beneath them was thin. But the rain had erased my tracks and all other signs of how I'd arrived here or where my friends might be.

Anxiously, I reached into my cuff and sagged in relief. The feather was barely warm. The storm had saved us.

A twig snapped and I froze.

"Aella?"

CHAPTER THREE

I spun, gasping with relief at the sight of a bedraggled Zayana leading a limping horse.

"I thought I was alone," I said.

"So did I," she said, rubbing her arms as she tried to warm herself. Her brown eyes were wide, flitting from one point to the next across the forest floor.

"Did you see what happened to Wing Ivo?" I asked.

She shook her head. Her attention still skittered across the landscape, her bottom lip trembling.

"Ivo?" she called.

I threw my hand up, shaking my head urgently. "Don't call! We're not out of danger yet!"

She rolled her eyes but at least her disdain seemed to shake her out of her anxiety. "What's worse? Being caught or being so lost that we never find our way out of this forest?"

"Being caught," I said firmly. A shiver of fear rushed through me along with memories of Osprey's agonized face and Juste's delighted one. I mustn't let him catch me. I mustn't let them ever see me again. "You have no idea what they'll do to me."

But I had to pause as a memory from the snake people seared itself across my mind.

The vision was of two young warriors, lost in a forest like this one. One of them was speaking to the other. We need to find the entrance to the undertrails in the forest. We can use them to get away from these strange intruders.

The other shook his head vehemently.

I blinked and it was gone. Just one of their memories. No wonder it was triggered when it was so close to what Zayana and I were fighting about right now.

"Wing Ivo!" she called again. Clearly, being lost was more terrifying to her than being caught.

I reached into my cuff, heart pounding, but to my relief, it was still just a dull warmth against my fingers.

I squinted at the sun, rising slowly in a streak of gold broken up by trunks of trees.

"Glorious Ingvar is southwest of here," I told Zayana. "And there are many settlements here in the south of Far Stones. We'll just chart a southwest course and we'll find a road or a town soon enough."

Her eyes lit with hope. "Have you traveled through this forest then?"

They faded with my reply. "No."

But what else was there to do?

We led our horses over the crumpled leaf carpet. It turned out I'd hurt my horse's mouth with my foolishness and Zayana's horse had a bad limp. Even if they'd been fine, we'd still have to navigate the thick trees and that meant walking. And it meant slow going. By noon, we both felt like we'd hardly made any progress at all and the worry I felt inside intensified with every moment that passed. I was going to be caught. And when I was caught, I was going to regret not finding some clever way to get away while I still could.

"Quite the chase we're giving Osprey," Zayana said. "A slow meander through the woods. A child could find us like this."

I held my tongue. Forests were difficult to navigate and the trees above us were thick. But wandering around in circles wasn't going to help us get away. Even if all my instincts were screaming at me to just run in any direction and not look back.

We rested at what we thought must be noon and ate a little of the bread from the saddlebags. It had stayed dry in its oil-cloth wrapping, unlike our cloaks and clothing. Despite the warmth of the day, I was chilled from being soaked through and I couldn't seem to warm myself. Worse, I felt as if someone was following us. And of course, someone was, though Os's feather remained cool to the touch.

I also had the strangest sensation that I was being drawn along, as if I was hearing voices just on the edge of sound, but when I walked over the next rise or around the next tree, they were gone.

I leaned against a stone structure we'd found and tried to stop worrying, running my hand down the unnaturally straight line of the stone. It felt almost as if it were cut by humans. Strange how nature could fool you from time to time.

Zayana began to hum from where she was around the curve of the rock. Surprised, I crept around the corner of the rock and stole a glance at her. She was dancing and humming to herself as her spirit-cardinal hovered in the air nearby. Her dance moved around him, not quite in a circle, more like a many-pointed star. With each pass, he seemed to brighten just a little. He'd grown since I'd met them. Now, he was about the size of my two hands together.

I watched her for a moment. How interesting. Osprey caressed his bird. Ivo gave his grand speeches. Zayana danced – and her dance was so graceful, she seemed almost to fly from point to point. It was hard to begrudge the Winged Empire praise for the delightful manifestations it produced. And despite loving my bees and finding a certain comfort in their contrary nature, I still felt a little ashamed that what came out of my heart was buzzing rage instead of this soaring beauty.

In my mind a mental image flared – one of my bees, reporting in. It was only a flash of my sister Raquella smiling over the edge of a steaming tin mug, but it was enough to make my heart leap. Raquella was alive out there somewhere and she had enough reason to smile. Warmth filled me at the thought.

And then another bee stole my vision. This time, I was very close to whoever was being watched. Close enough to see that he was changing the dressing on a blood-soaked bandage. His dark skin was taut over corded muscles that flexed tight when he flinched from the pain. I still couldn't see his face, but I knew who it was before the hand snatched toward my bee and his voice carried to me.

"What are you doing here, little bee? Where is your keeper?"

I gasped and the vision shattered. Osprey. I'd thought I'd left my bee with Juste but had it attached itself to Osprey instead?

I cleared my throat, as my vision returned to Zayana. "We should keep going."

Her bird flared as she startled, his red light splashing over the rock – so bright that it nearly blinded me. But it didn't blind me completely. Instead, it showed very faint markings in the stone formation. So faint and worn that I couldn't see them at all under the lichen and could barely make them out in Flame's bright light.

"Did you see that?" I asked, hurrying to trace my finger over the markings.

"I saw nothing."

"It was here …" I ran my fingers further along it, but if the markings meant something, I couldn't make it out. My brow furrowed as I studied them.

"Look, what you saw just now … can you keep it between us?" Zayana twisted her hands together nervously. "It's not precisely forbidden, but the Wings prefer that I use words to invoke traits in Flame. And they are right, of course. Words have great power. Look at how calling yourselves revolutionaries has changed you and Ivo, pitting you against the authorities. Your words are so powerful that I doubt you could wipe them away even if you changed your mind and dropped the name tomorrow. And that's why the other Wings would frown on such an unorthodox approach. But you see, the dancing … it is my words. It's my way of showing my heart."

I was barely listening.

As she spoke, a vision flashed over my eyes. A second vision of those two young warriors standing before this stone. Only that mossy fallen log hadn't been there and the top of the stone had been higher. I scrambled toward the spot where they paused before it and as I watched them caress the door, I wrenched the log from in front of it away. It crumbled, stinking of old rot, insect eggs tumbling from the masses.

This was the first time I'd ever been able to move while having one of their visions. Dizziness washed over me and I fought it, concentrating.

Something rumbled in the distance – more thunder, perhaps.

"Are you listening?" Zayana asked.

"I'm great at keeping secrets," I said as I leaned down and dug at the moss and loose earth that blocked what I just knew was a door. "You can trust me."

"Well, you kept from me the secret that you and Ivo were working against the crown prince," she said huffily. "You got me entangled in something I didn't choose, and I don't want!"

"Can you shine the light of that bird over here?" I asked. "I think I see something."

"Flame is not a torch to be used to light your path!" But her bird flared and I could see better.

It was a door! I could see the outline of it. I pulled my belt knife out and traced the line of it through the lichen. A door to the undertrails – whatever those were. A little shiver stole over me at the thrill of it. My visions were true. And the one I'd seen was actually helpful. That meant the general was out there somewhere, too.

This must be why the Hissan had told Juste to keep me close. They would likely envision me sharing these insights with him, guiding his path along the way. Only because of his cowardice, this help was mine now, instead of his.

I shook my head.

I had an advantage that I'd give up in a heartbeat if I could. But I'd be a fool not to use it, wouldn't I?

I began to scrape the lichen off the rock, but even when I

removed a patch, the markings were too faint to see what was under it. Only Flame's brilliant scarlet light brought out dark shadows that showed the outlines of what had been there before.

My vision came back. The warriors standing here, with straight backs and flowing hair. One touched a spot at the top right corner. Then another spot at waist height – which was about where the door reached the ground now.

I dropped to my knees, fingers dancing along the rock as I tried to find the same spot.

"It's like you aren't even listening to me, Aella. I saw a tree growing out of the fallen remains of two other trees. It's a clear sign that I'm on the wrong path."

I looked up at that. "I'm listening. You don't want to go against the crown prince. And now you're stuck with us."

"Yes." She seemed almost relieved. "That's exactly my problem."

"And you think that if you can find some way to get back to them and please them, then they won't harm your sister, who they have as a captive."

"Yes!"

"You're wrong." This spot. I was nearly sure of it. I scraped the lichen off to mark the place. "I tried that, and they just continued to torment my family."

"Yes, but you're … difficult. Enraging. The crown prince hates you in particular."

I met her eyes. "And do you think he wouldn't hate you if you could just find a way to please him? He slit the throats of his own Claws and used their blood to fight the Forbidding back. He'd slit yours just as easily."

She crossed her arms. "I'm not asking to be exalted to a named position, Aella. I just don't want to be on the run from the Empire. I'll travel with you, but if Osprey comes for us again, I plan to let him find me. It was a mistake to run with you and Ivo. A terrible risk that I shouldn't have taken."

Well, that explained all the calling in the forest even after I'd warned her.

"If you keep second-guessing yourself like that, your bird will stay tiny. You need to take a risk once in a while, Zayana. You know that we're right. That what we're doing is the right thing. You should be on our side."

I tried to tap one symbol and then the other. Nothing. I frowned.

She scoffed. "Running for your lives from the most powerful Empire of the world is the 'right thing'? Tell yourself whatever you want, Aella, but you're all fools. The only way to deal with the Empire of War and Wings is to keep your head down and your mouth shut, and you don't seem capable of either of those things."

I stretched, reaching to touch both symbols at once as the rain began again, pouring so suddenly from the sky that Zayana let out a little shriek. Her bird disappeared.

The moment my hands touched both spots, the lichen-encrusted door swung inward with a groan. The smell of mildew and decay swirled out to meet us.

"See?" I said through the pouring rain. "I am capable of other things. I just opened a secret door."

CHAPTER FOUR

"I'm not going in there." Zayana looked mulish. "The horses won't even fit."

"I think there are tunnels here that lead other places," I said hopefully.

She looked up at the sky and I followed her gaze, worried about what she was seeing. Had Osprey found us? I slapped my hand to the leather cuff, but it wasn't hot enough for that and when I looked back, Zayana was just shaking her head.

"You, Aella, are the most head-strong, frustrating girl on the planet. There is a hidden moldy door that leads into darkness. You don't know where it goes. But you're certain that's the path. Meanwhile, we have horses and a clear plan out here."

"A clear plan? We've taken all day to go maybe a couple of miles. Maybe. We're not exactly lost, but it's close. This door might be a chance for something better."

Plus, maybe it would be a chance to stay clear of the one hunting me, in particular. I clenched my jaw and forced that fear from my mind.

"Or, the door will close behind us when we go inside and we'll be trapped in a stone room to die together," Zayana said. She had mounted her horse while we spoke, as if to emphasize her conclusion.

"I just want to look inside," I pressed. "Come look with me."

"Absolutely not."

"Well, I'll look, then."

It wasn't easy to get in the door. Not only was the top half narrow, but the ground fell abruptly into the open door. I ended up going in backward, legs dangling into the hole until they found the ground. My cloak was muddy by the time I got into the doorway, wrinkling my nose at the mildew scent of the place.

I opened my palm in the darkness.

"Bees?"

They poured into my palm like honey, golden and liquid, their buzz almost a purr. Oh, look who is so well behaved now? I almost rolled my eyes, but I was too occupied with wonder.

"Let's see what we have here!"

I was in a little room. It was obviously made by the Hissan people – it had their endless snake motif everywhere – along the edge of the floors, crawling up to unlit sconces and wrapping up the pedestal in the center of the little room right before me. I walked up to the pedestal and brushed dust away from a plaque sitting on it. I could not read the unfamiliar words on the plaque but after a moment, I recognized the shape. It was a map of Far Stones. A lot more map than I was used to. It stretched deep into the lands taken by the Forbidding, lands we didn't even know the shape of.

There were carved symbols on various points of the map. One that must be where we were – just a little larger than the rest. And if it was our location shown there then we'd made very little progress traveling today. There were other points, too. Some of them were far from the known parts of the continent, deep into the tangled Forbidding north of here. Others, were not far from locations I knew. There was one near the great bridge that led to Far Reach. Another near Far Port. Another yet that was a few miles – if the scale was accurate – from one of the Pincher Towers. There were dozens of locations on both the known and unknown portions of the Far Stones continent. There was even one close to Glorious Ingvar.

Now, if I could just have another vision showing me how to make this next part work. I closed my eyes and gritted my teeth. Nothing. Okay. I'd have to work this out for myself.

I looked up to where three paths branched out from the room I was in and then back to the plaque where three lines led out from this marker to three other markers. One of them was inland from Astar Harbor. It had a line going from it to Glorious Ingvar – or close to that city. I looked back up at the branching trails. Easy enough. Take the trail on the left and we'd get there, right?

I felt my heart pounding at that. I hadn't been wrong. I was sure of it. These undertrails really could take us where we needed to go. And Osprey couldn't hunt us while we were in here. He wouldn't even know this place existed. We could meet Ivo in Ingvar and find those records and if we were really lucky, we might even find that one of these trails led to where the general was held – and then we'd rescue him and raise our army. I was already halfway through the daydream when Zayana called into the little room.

"Are you dead?"

"Not yet."

I scrambled out of the door, up the bank of crumbling earth. Clearly, I was more terrified of being caught than I was of walking underground.

"I think that there are trails here, under the ground," I said. "We can go almost all the way to Glorious Ingvar using them! No rain. No Osprey. No chance of being caught."

She raised a hand with a skeptical look on her face. "Tunnel collapses." She turned a finger down. "Poisonous gases." Another finger. "No water." Another. "No air." A fourth finger. "No way out when we get there." That was the last finger. She stuck up her thumb and immediately pushed it down, too. "No light if our magic doesn't work. Oh, and we might get lost with no way to navigate. And it might take longer than it would out here. We could wander lost until we die. There's no way I'm going in there."

I swallowed. I couldn't leave her here, but my plan was better.

"Without me, you can't navigate," I said. "You don't know this land, and your woodcraft is terrible."

Her face went stony.

I crossed my arms. "And I'm taking this underground trail."

"At least think it through, you stubborn girl!" Her cheeks flushed with emotion.

"I have. And I'm going."

I pulled the saddlebags and saddle from my horse, setting them on the ground, and began to remove the bridle. She nickered happily at the freedom.

The problem was, Zayana wasn't wrong. Any one of those things could happen. I wasn't even sure this was a good idea, but what else was I going to do? I felt this constant pressure weighing on me, like it was up to me to turn everything right and I hadn't done it yet. And that meant that I needed to take some risks, right? I needed to try things other people hadn't tried. I needed to succeed, or everything would be lost.

"Stubborn and nonsensical," Zayana said. Were those tears I heard in her voice?

I patted my horse's nose as I removed her bit. "There's a girl. Hopefully, you can find your way home."

I opened the saddlebags and rummaged in them, taking out the sack of food and the waterskin. There was nothing else in them, so I slung the rope holding the waterskin over my shoulder and made my way back to the entrance.

I didn't say goodbye to Zayana as I slid into the tunnel again. She would come with me. I knew it. Cautious as she was, worried as she was, she was someone who followed a leader and I was that leader.

I studied the map as I waited for her. Was this as simple as it appeared? It seemed straightforward enough. Hopefully, I was guessing correctly.

We just had to make the trek on foot and in soaking clothes and in the dark. No problem, right?

I opened my palm and watched as my bees spun round and round to make a globe over it. They would light my way. I felt a flicker of uncertainty but quickly suppressed it. If I spent my time worrying about what could go wrong, I'd be just like Zayana.

"Nice work, you fuzzy creatures," I whispered to them. "Now, be bright and beautiful!"

I heard the sound of slipping and quiet cursing. I smiled but I didn't turn. No need to spook her before she was fully committed.

Okay, time to go. Fixing the map in my mind, I strode toward the correct entrance to the tunnels. Each was shaped – horrifically – like the mouth of a snake, its incisors pointed downward. The yawning gapes of their mouths were pitch black – even the light of my bees didn't penetrate the dark – which was worrisome. It was just like the Hissan to make you feel like you were being swallowed up into the belly of a snake when you were only trying to travel somewhere. But I couldn't complain too much. They'd brought me here. And this was a chance that had potential.

I stumbled right before I reached the door and a heavy memory of those warriors weighed on me again.

"I always hate this part," one of the warriors said with a shudder. He was looking at the door on the right. "It feels as though it robs me of the years."

"An illusion, brother. It will speed you on your path and honor the Great Snake. Just step through quickly before you talk yourself out if it."

Zayana caught my elbow in a muddy hand and I flickered back to real life.

"Don't change your mind on me now," she said wryly. "I'm already coated in mud."

"Of course not," I agreed, sharing a grim smile with her. "Are you ready?"

"You're a terrible influence on me."

I took that as a yes and stepped into the mouth of the carved adder.

The very air grabbed a hold of me once my foot crossed the threshold, seeming to fold me into it – almost as if I really was being swallowed. I held my breath as Zayana gasped beside me.

“I’m already regretting this, bee girl!”

The ground under us shuddered and folded again and then my bees went dark.

CHAPTER FIVE

"Bees!" I whispered. "Come back to me!"

I could still feel their buzz in my chest, but my vision was completely dark. Zayana clung to my elbow and I reached up and grabbed her hand with my free hand. If she was speaking to me, I couldn't hear it. If she was breathing, I couldn't hear it.

The ground rumbled again and that feeling of folding seemed to pull me along, but it was as if a candle had gone out in the blackest of nights, as if I was adrift in the depths of a sky without stars. A prayer broke from my heart.

Flight of wind protect us, mercy of the skies fly over us, give us peace and protection, let us soar from this terror on the wings of eagles.

I found myself repeating it aloud. There was something about prayer that made me feel braver. As if just acknowledging that there was something in control beyond me was a step toward believing it could keep me safe.

"Skies send mercy. Wrap us in your depths cloud upon cloud, hold us fast with the might of your winds."

Something shifted in the folding.

I grew bolder in my prayer.

"In the ever-changing nature of life, in the storms and

stillness, shine your light on us."

The folding became faster and with it, the buzz in my chest increased until I could barely hear my own words as I said, "Make us fast as we ride your zephyrs, make us pure as we bathe in your rays."

The rumbling was constant as if my words had sped everything up. Was it possible that I was somehow invoking this passage like we invoked our manifestations?

I spoke again.

"Bind us together like your flocks of birds and your clouds of bees."

I felt Zayana's hand pressed against mine and tried to will confidence into her. She was going to be so mad when we came out again.

It felt like a gathering now, like when dough is kneaded – folded first and then forced back on itself. We were being kneaded. Pain flared inside me as memories bubbled up to the surface in little flickers and then dissipated. Each flicker carried an aftertaste of what I'd felt when those memories were made. The sweetness of my mother singing over me ran right into the searing rawness of watching my father killed before my eyes. The warmth of my siblings' smiles crashed into the sharp fear of being snatched in the air by a snake. And in it all, the buzz of the bees carried on and the folding and kneading continued.

It was like being reshaped. It was not a comfortable feeling at all.

I reached with my heart toward the skies. I reached and hoped there really was something deep, deep, deep in the endless blue who guarded us like a father and loved us like a mother and would reach down and contain me so I didn't run out of myself like an uncooked yolk from an egg.

And then I spoke. Because if speaking into a manifestation caused order to form from chaos, then maybe I could form some order here, too.

"Bear us to our destination with speed, but leave us whole," I said, channeling all my hope into my words. "Do not shatter our shells or leak our yolks out. We are brave and determined. We are relentless. We are filled up to the brim with compassion. Let us thrive! Do not break us. Bear us out of this darkness."

The rumbling slowed. And the folding grew fainter and then – as if a door had been opened – the wind rushed into my lungs and light burst across my vision.

I took a step forward, still clutching Zayana's hand – but there was something very still about the moment. As if I was steady within myself with no need to speak or act. It lasted only the blink of an eye but in that blink, I felt like I had been made new, as if that kneading had pulled together frayed edges and shaped me into something slightly sleeker, slightly more ordered, slightly bolder.

I swallowed and the moment was over. The buzz of my bees returned and they roared back into a globe in front of me.

"You're back!" I whispered to them. "Welcome back."

I took another step forward, pulling Zayana with me and with a lurch, I realized I had crossed the threshold through the snake's mouth and back into the little room.

We hadn't gone anywhere at all. And yet, I felt as if days had passed. I wobbled unsteadily and turned to Zayana.

She had a curious look on her face. She opened her mouth

and then shut it again, swallowing visibly before she whispered, "Someone shut the door."

I let go of her hand and scrambled past the plaque to the door. It was completely shut. Stranger yet, there was no muddy trail where we had come in. I spun to look at Zayana and found her staring up at the ceiling.

Oh.

There was a small hole in the ceiling, lighting the room. That had not been there before. My eyes fell on the plaque and I gasped. The signs on the map had changed. The larger sign had been near to Karkatua before. But now, the larger sign was inland from Astar Harbor. That must be where we were now.

I swallowed as the realization settled over me. We had moved. We'd moved in minutes a distance that should have taken days. But now I realized what the snake warriors had meant when they said that they "hated that part" because as I looked up to the center snake with its wide yawning mouth, I knew I'd have to go into the belly of the snake again. Sweat formed on my brow and I swallowed down a stab of fear.

"Did we … move?" Zayana asked. Her hands were trembling. "It took me apart and stitched me back together and I don't think I like it at all."

I had to clear my throat before I could speak. "I think we're halfway to Glorious Ingvar. It was like a magic portal in a Forbidding Tale. Look."

I pointed to the map on the plaque and Zayana looked at it and then at me. "I can't read the words."

"Neither can I. I'm just judging by the shape of the continent. Did you speak while we were … traveling?"

She shook her head. "I won't be speaking this time, either."

My eyebrows rose in surprise, but her features took on a firm look. Who would have thought that Zayana could be so relentless? It must be tough to be so far from everything she knew.

I took a deep breath. "I think it's better if we hold hands."

She let me take her hand and then we stepped up to the center door. The one that the map showed leading to the spot just outside Glorious Ingvar. We hesitated.

"We could travel the rest of the way on foot," I offered. "We've already saved ourselves days of travel."

She shook her head determinedly but although I waited for her to say something, she remained steadfastly silent.

"Relentless," I said and I stepped over the threshold, flinching as the air folded me in and everything went dark again.

This time, when the floor began to rumble and the folding started, I didn't hesitate. I lifted my heart to the skies and spoke order into the chaos.

"Bear us quickly to our destination but bear us whole and full. Do not let us break or crumble, fade or snap under your folding. We want to be strong and whole. We want to be brave and kind."

I couldn't think of what else to say, but I didn't need to say anything more. The folding began – faster this time. I felt the pull and squeeze of it. Memories bubbled up with their emotions and were folded back in, but I had a strange sensation that I was having trouble holding onto even as the thoughts formed. Were all of those memories mine? Or was it reaching in and pulling up memories I'd been given by the Hissan and folding those in, too? My mind was too busy to analyze it, but my instincts made me shiver at the thought.

It was a matter of seconds until the heaving and folding stopped. But it felt like hours. Emotions I didn't want and memories I had tried to hold at bay warred in me, leaving me breathless and wrung out like a rag. When – finally – they were done, I was left gasping, my chest heaving, tears leaking down my face. The first thing I heard was a muffled sob as we stepped together across the threshold. Zayana clung to my hand, and the moment we were clear, she wrenched her hand away, hiding her face as she sobbed.

Feeling dazed, I wrapped her into a hug and tried to shake my head clear.

Well. You wouldn't use those every day, would you? Not even if they saved you months of travel.

"Never again," Zayana gasped through her tears.

I didn't echo her. Who knew what might come next? But when I summoned my bees, I was astonished to realize that they were brighter than before. I blew on them, and they seemed to warm with my breath.

"Do you feel – energetic?" I asked Zayana warily.

She frowned. "I shouldn't feel that way. But I do." She opened her palms and Flame appeared. "He's brighter."

He was larger, too.

I looked over my shoulder at the three yawning mouths with suspicion. What were those things? Perhaps, I shouldn't have leapt into unknown magic. Anything could have happened – maybe even something far worse than this.

Swallowing, I made my way across the floor. The room was

filled with rotting leaves. It was easy to see why. The hole in the top of the structure that lit this room was as wide as my fist and debris fell into the room easily, forming a rotting pile around the plaque. No one had used these undertrails in a very long time.

I frowned. Why would that be? They seemed like something that Ixtap would want to leverage.

I made my way through the drifting leaves to the door and placed my hands on the symbols that had opened the door on the other side.

Nothing happened.

My heart sped up as fear tasted acid in my mouth. I looked back at the yawning mouths.

I did not want to go back in there.

"Don't tell me that we're stuck," Zayana said. She sounded frantic.

I tried to look calm, despite my racing heart and the skittering of my bees in response. Okay, calmly now, Aella. Look for another option.

I looked up at the ceiling. A fist-sized hole. Could we dig it wider? It was ringed in carefully dressed stone. That would be a no. Without tools, we couldn't possibly move it. I swallowed.

A vision filled my eyes – sent from one of my bees.

Ixtap – dressed in finery – at a feast on the shore of the ocean. He raised his goblet in a toast to cheers all around him. They were celebrating something. Behind him, in the ocean, the silhouette of many ships bobbed on the waves. I fought against the vision, my body instinctually bucking against the invasion into my mind. More than ever, I hated that the snake people had implanted a part of themselves in me. I hated that they could give me memories and thoughts. We were stuck here and that was all my fault, but it didn't keep me from feeling resentful of them. I pushed the vision aside.

Drawing in a long breath, I focused. We needed a plan.

Okay, so maybe there were different symbols for different doors. I tried a few at random. Nothing.

"We really are stuck." Zayana said hopelessly. She walked to the side of the room, put her back to the circular wall of the round room, placed her head in her hands, and began to silently sob.

I couldn't blame her. I felt like crying, too. After all that, to think we might have to do it over again having accomplished nothing … I couldn't bear the thought.

CHAPTER SIX

The energy I'd felt before seemed to be draining away as the minutes ticked by. I tried more door combinations. I tried feeling the sides of the room looking for a way out. Above us, the light in the fist-sized hole faded until it was gone.

"This is what we get for defying the Empire," Zayana said hopelessly. Her face was smeared with tears and dust.

I spun to face her. "What is what we get? What?"

"Punishment. Disaster. What did you expect by defying them?"

I crossed my arms and leaned down so she could see me in the last shreds of fading light. Without meaning to, I manifested bees. Two of them. They spun glowing spirals around us as I spoke.

"I've been trying and trying to tell you, Zayana. When are you going to listen? Your loyalty to the Empire is misplaced. They've taken everything from you."

"Not my sister." Her face was tear streaked in the light of my bees. "She's alive, living with patrons."

"So that they can hold her over your head and use you? Or, so they can use her later?"

"She's already going to pay a price because of what you and

Wing Ivo did!"

"Because we saved a city from enemies? Think about that. Your sister is going to pay a price because you helped two people save an Imperial city from invasion. Because we saved little children from being murdered in their homes? Does that sound right to you?"

"It doesn't matter if it's right. It matters that it is. I can't change it, so I have to live under it."

I huffed and stood up again. If I couldn't get this idea through her head, I couldn't work with her. She'd seemed so close to understanding when we left the snake temple but she kept getting tangled up again in her loyalty to the Empire.

"I'm afraid, too, okay?" I said, trying to put my whole heart into this explanation. "Juste Montpetit wants my family dead – specifically. He wants to torture me – specifically. It's not a vague, general, maybe threat. It's a specific one. But why should I be afraid of him? Why should I let him have that kind of power over me? You know what? I'm angry. I'm angry all the time because I feel so powerless and even that isn't enough. So, instead of being just angry and just scared, I'm doing something about it. I'm joining this revolution of Wing Ivo's and I'm going to act because one way or another none of us gets out of this life alive. We all die eventually. Why spend all my time afraid of it and trying to cling to the scraps they'll give me? I won't do that. I'd rather fight for freedom – even if I lose – than die with their boot on my neck."

"You're a fool." Her words were faint.

"Then come be a fool with me." I pled. "You need to finally make a decision. I'm not bringing you with me if you aren't on our side. You can go back to pretending that everything is fine with the Empire and that you can have a life under their rule. Or you can come with me and if you come with me, then I don't want to see any more waffling. I want to see some courage."

She frowned and I turned my back on her, striding to stand in front of the three yawning mouths as she made up her mind.

It seemed to take forever. I had to bite my lip to keep from tapping a foot or turning around to see if she'd gone to sleep. Above me, in the tiny window to the sky, the stars shone bright and the coolness of night descended into the little underground room. It felt like hours that I'd stood there waiting. But better this than a knife in my back the first time we saw a Claw patrol. Better to wait than to have her signaling Osprey the next time he flew over us.

I reached into the leather cuff and touched Os's feather. It was stone cold. I stroked it gently. What did cold mean? It was always warm. Should I be worried about Osprey?

Calm down, Aella. The waiting is getting to you.

I almost sighed with relief when scarlet light flared behind me, and Zayana's whisper-soft footsteps brought her to join me. She stood a full head shorter than me. Delicate and beautiful, just like her bird, but her eyes had a bold look in them when she turned to face me.

"This isn't for you, you know."

I smirked. "Of course not."

"Which of these horrible snakes swallows us this time?" She held her chin high like she was trying to keep from shuddering.

"None of them."

I turned to the plaque and followed a hunch that had been

growing as I waited. I touched the symbol on the map that marked the spot where our room was and heard the grinding of stone on stone as the door swung open on its own.

"Did you know it would do that all along?" Zayana asked.

I shook my head. "Sometimes you have to follow a hunch and take a risk."

She took a big breath and sighed.

"Let's go out and conquer," I said.

She snorted a disbelieving laugh, but she followed me out of the door and into the crisp night. The door swung shut behind us with a faint click. In the darkness, it was hard to see much of our surroundings. There were tall rocks arranged around us in a semi-circle and out past them were trees.

Something moved in the trees and I felt a stab of fear in my gut. Was it a tentacle of Forbidding? I swallowed down fear. After all, I couldn't demand that Zayana be brave if I wasn't brave myself.

"Let's spend the night in this stone circle," I suggested. "We can build a fire here."

Zayana nodded, her eyes fearful as she peered into the darkness. We built our fire in silence and huddled up against the nearest stone before dropping into a fitful, uncomfortable sleep.

I woke to a sense that something was wrong.

I remained motionless, letting my eyes flick open and trying to study our surroundings without twitching. Was that a ghost of a movement?

I held my breath, listening. There were no more sounds to

give me a clue of what I'd heard, but there was still the sense that something was following us. I woke Zayana hurriedly and we kicked out the fire and began to move through the darkness, using our manifestations to light the way.

"I don't think this is wise," she'd objected. "We won't be able to see your Forbidding if it's here and we don't know where we're going."

But whether it was by luck or the skies favored us, we stumbled onto an old road moments later. It was grown over with long grass and low tree branches, but it was passable. We hurried down the road, sticking close together. By the time dawn lit the sky, we had reached a crossroads where a wide, well-traveled road intersected it. I put the glimmer of gold to our backs and we began the tired march toward Glorious Ingvar in the west.

All day, I felt eyes on my back. I jumped at every snapped stick or shift in the wind until Zayana began to jump with me. We passed two towns before I agreed to stop and purchase a little food. We passed two more before the light began to fade again. The people in the last town had told us it would take another long day to reach Glorious Ingvar, so we found a quiet glen along the road to stay for the night.

"I'm too tired to go farther tonight," Zayana had said as she persuaded me to build a fire there. "We have shaved days off our travel time. Let's not waste that advantage by running ourselves into the ground. We won't want to reach the city exhausted."

I waited long minutes, watching the road behind us before I agreed to the fire. The road had been busy all day but as night drew near, there was only a lone horse which quickly walked by, its rider too intent on reaching a town to even glance our way.

"Okay, we can camp for half the night," I agreed. "Then back to the road."

"Half a night," Zayana repeated, shaking her head. "We are likely days ahead of Wing Ivo and yet you won't even sleep a full night!"

But I couldn't explain this feeling of being hunted. I checked the cuff constantly to feel the feather, but it wasn't Osprey who was close by. It was someone else. Could he have sent Claws after us, too?

Reluctantly, I settled with Zayana next to the fire and joined her in eating the rest of the food we'd bought in the village. Together, we spoke to our manifestations, and then together we tried to get comfortable by the fire. We took opposite sides to it this time, each of us absorbed in our own thoughts.

"Why do they call the city 'Glorious Ingvar?'" she asked.

"It was the first place settlers landed when they arrived in the Far Stones," I said with a yawn. "Conquerors might be a better word. But they found no people here. Just the Forbidding. They fought it back, though it killed half of them and wrecked their ship, seizing it from the waves. They held the rocky piece of coast, battling back the Forbidding until another ship came to help them. By the time it arrived, nine in ten of the men who had arrived on the shores were dead. So, they named the beach after an old story – the story of the Ishanians who were conquered three centuries ago by the Winged Empire. They called their underworld Ingvar."

"Are you saying that this city's name translated is 'Glorious Hell'?"

I nodded. "And that's all you need to know about the Far Stones."

She yawned. “I suppose it is.”

I fell asleep dreaming fitfully of blood on a rocky ocean shore. And I awoke just as I had the night before with the sense that there was someone else nearby. I stayed motionless, barely squinting my eyes open.

CHAPTER SEVEN

A twig snapped just behind me and before I could sit up, a hand clamped over my mouth. I grabbed at the wrist, my heart pounding, terror clawing up my throat. They were man's hands. Rough. Hairy. Panic coursed through me. He'd found me. Osprey had found me.

"Shh." The whisper in my ear was so faint that I could barely hear it. "Easy now, Shrikeling."

Relief filled me, mixing with a sense of joy so strong it nearly choked me. The hand loosened as I spun, jaw dropping.

My brother Retger's intense eyes stared back at me as he wrapped me into a hug.

"Retger. I must be dreaming." It was all I could do to keep from sobbing with relief, but I couldn't help the suppressed emotions that rippled through me. I pressed my face into his shoulder.

He let me stay there a moment before tugging me away from where Zayana slept. I followed him into the moonlit shadows.

"How did you find me?" I asked.

"I've been tracking you since a few days after they took you," he whispered. "I lost you at Vlaren but I thought I'd found you again in Karkatua. I swore I saw you on the city walls during the fighting."

"You did!" I gasped. "I thought I saw Oska!"

"He was with me as far as Karkatua. I had to leave him there. He's gathering supplies for the family. But let me tell the story!" He laughed softly. He had a satchel at his side and as he spoke, he drew out a flask and handed it to me. I drank as he spoke – apple cider. A rare treat for us. "I followed a Wing to a large house and thought I saw a glimpse of you escaping through the window, but I wasn't fast enough and by the time I turned the corner, you were gone. I had to dig deep after that – dig into contacts I have in the area."

"The Single Wing?" I asked and his eyebrows shot up.

"Did the old man tell you about that?" He looked eager.

"Not the details, just the name." I bit my lip. "Retger, he … I watched him die."

My brother cursed, leaning back from me to rub a hand over his face as he cursed again. "We'd hoped … I'd thought…" He shook his head as if dismissing his thoughts. "I'll get you out of here, Shrikeling. Before they kill you, too. Here. Eat something. You're wasting away."

He took the flask and handed me an oil-cloth wrapped cake. I unwrapped the cloth and dug in hungrily. The smell and taste of honey nearly made me shut my eyes in joy, but I tried to stay focused as I chewed.

"How are the others? Are they safe?"

He shrugged. "They were when I left. Abghar was leading them into the Forbidding. They will carve out a safe space there and we will join them as soon as we can get back. Are you ready to ride now? Skies, it's good to see you alive! I brought a spare horse. Let me tell you, that was tricky through those snake mouths."

"How … how did you know which path I took?" I licked the crumbs from my fingers, wishing I had another cake. It had been like a taste of home.

He grinned proudly. "Followed your tracks into that underground room. Had to convince the horses to duck and crawl into it. I'm not as good with horses as Oska is but you'd be surprised by what little tricks we pick up as blacksmiths. Someone has to shoe these beasts. I used every trick I knew to get them in there. Then, I followed the scuffs of your boots on the floor through the right snake mouth twice. The last door had me tricked, but I figured it out after a minute."

I shook my head. "You're amazing."

He nudged me playfully with an elbow, digging into his bag again.

"We aren't going back that way, Shrikeling. We'll ride. That thing shook me up inside and I don't want to do that again. Now, come on. Your minder will miss you if we don't leave soon."

I shot a look back to Zayana sleeping in the moonlight and then back to Retger again. All I ever wanted was for my family to be safe. It was like fruit on top of cake that I might be able to go with them. For a moment, I let myself believe I could go. I let myself hope for just a minute that I could leave all this behind and just be Aella of House Shrike again.

But I knew better than that. Too much had changed. I was Aella of House Apidae now.

"I can't, Retger," I whispered. "I wish I could, but I can't."

"Do you realize what it took to find you?" He didn't sound angry, just surprised. "I don't know how easy it will be to do it again."

"I still can't believe that you managed it at all."

"We all would have come, Shrikeling." His eyes were earnest. What he drew out of the bag now was a scarf – warm but light in the finest spun white wool. I knew the craftsmanship. This was one of Helissa's scarves. She sold them at the larger markets in the autumn. "We would have fought through all of the Forbidding to get to you. You have to know that. They sent me because they knew I could do it myself, but if it needed all of us, we all would have come."

"Are they all … is everyone in the family still alive? No one died when the Claws took Far Reach?"

He nodded. "Alect walks with a limp now and Helissa's pretty face has a scar to give it some character. But we all survived. Except the old man, I guess. We'll erect a monument for him with a shrike totem. He'll like that. Here," he said as he handed me the scarf, "Helissa sent this for you."

"And you can survive out there? In the Forbidding?"

"We're House Shrike, Aella. We're relentless. You know that."

I nodded along with him, winding the warm scarf around my neck. "That's why I can't go back. I'm being hunted by more than just you, Retger. I'm being hunted by one of the Winged Empire's top Wings and he will drag me back to the crown prince one way or another."

No need to say why was there? I wasn't going to marry Juste. I'd rather slash my own throat. He would torture me in every way he could think of – both mentally and physically. I knew enough to know that.

"I'd like to see him try," Retger said, flexing his powerful blacksmith-arms almost unconsciously. "I can outride any man there is and outfight at least half of them. I'll watch your back Shrikeling, have no fear!"

It was so tempting. I could see us riding like the wind – maybe even taking the undertrails again – and leaving Osprey confused and lost. We could be free. We could join the rest of the family and I could be with my siblings and their children. We could carve a life for ourselves. And then what? What happened when the Winged Empire found us again? What happened when we ran out of necessary supplies? What happened when someone was injured or hurt or if the Forbidding got too strong for us? What then? Just running away wouldn't change things. It couldn't.

"I want you all to be safe. But more than that, I want you to be free. To have weapons to defend yourselves," I said.

"We had a hidden stash."

"To be able to get more when those are broken or old. To be able to get supplies as needed without being in hiding. To say what you want without fear of retribution. To raise the little ones to love freedom and our way of living."

"We can have that." He was trying to convince me. He put his hands on my upper arms as if he wished he could physically lift me and fly me away with him. Like Osprey could.

"We can't. Not while the Empire has Far Stones. Not while all our trade goes through them. Not while they rule with an iron fist."

"That's why there's a Single Wing, Aella. To fight for that." His earnestness was almost pleading now.

"And who is going to fight with them?"

He clenched his jaw in agreement, looking away.

"You know that, Retger. And you probably think it isn't worth talking about because I'm too young."

"Exactly." He met my eyes again. His fire raging against my fire. We were both too stubborn to back down.

"But I've met the Single Wing. I know they're out there. We can fight together."

"Having a few passionate people on your side doesn't fix things. And even if it did, that would be a talk for grown men to have, Aella, not teen girls." His brown eyes were pleading now.

I crossed my arms over my chest. My whispers growing louder with my frustration.

"It's a discussion for me to have because I'm part of this now." My bees buzzed louder within my chest. One of them slipped out of my control, buzzing frantically around us, bumping into shoulders and ears in its enthusiasm. "I'm a symbol to them because of the bees. A spark to ignite the flame."

"They want to use you?" He sounded appalled. His hands dropped from my arms and one ran through his tangled curls.

"They want to fight with me! And we need a general, Retger. And I know exactly where to find one. Well, maybe not exactly, but I know there is one stashed in a tower around here. And we are going to Glorious Ingvar to read the old records and find out where the tower is."

"You sound crazy," he said, running his hand over his face as if he could make me see sense just by looking all angst-filled and haunted. "Are you even listening to yourself?"

"Yes. I am." I was getting frustrated now. "I've been telling myself this while I fled forest fires and snake manifestations and the original residents of this land."

"What?"

Three more bees poured out of my hands and flew dizzying rings around us.

"I've been telling myself this while I was tortured and mocked and pledged in marriage against my will to Juste Montpetit."

"What?" This time, his word sounded furious. The hands came down and his brown eyes burned bright in the moonlight.

"I might sound crazy, but only because I know things most people don't know and I've seen things they can't see and that means I have a different way of looking at all the rest. It's not crazy, Retger. It's accurate. Which is why I have to keep going. Even though I want to come home with you. Even though I want to see everyone again. Even though it might seem like there's nothing more that I could possibly want, I do want something more – I want to give my family freedom, and to do that, I have to fight this fight and I have to win, Retger. It's me against the Winged Empire and it will never stop until one of us wins and the other dies."

He blew a long breath out, shaking his head, but I kept talking.

"That's why I can't go with you. Because it would be selfish. It could spell the end of our family, and even if the Wing didn't hunt me down and kill our family trying to get me, I would still know that I could have helped to give you all a future, but I was too scared to try. I can't do that, Retger. I have to stay and fight. Even if I seem too young to you. I'm not. I'm growing up fast."

He was quiet for long moments as my bees hummed and danced around him.

"Fine," he said, eventually, and when he looked up his jaw

was clenched with determination. "But at least tell me we can do it on horseback. I don't want to let this pair go free when I've fought so hard to bring them here."

I hugged him suddenly and fiercely and he grunted hard.

"Thank you, Retger!" I said.

"At least let me get some sleep before dawn," he grumbled. He was always grumbly when he was trying to hide strong emotions.

"You were the one who was going to drag me out of bed!" I laughed.

"What bed?" he muttered, following me back to the low-burning fire. He unsaddled the horses while I stoked the fire but my heart was light and happy. Retger was here and he was going to help me get to Glorious Ingvar and free the general. What could be better than that?

I fell asleep happier than I'd been since I'd been taken from my home. My dreams were full of my family, sweet and fleeting. I melted into them, savoring every dream moment and feeling happy and at peace, knowing I would wake to family and an ally.

Instead, I woke to my leather cuff burning.

CHAPTER EIGHT

"He's here!" I cried, scrambling up to my feet and making sure the cloak was wrapped around me and the hood was over my head. "Zayana, wake up! Wake up! He's here!"

Her eyes popped open and she was on her feet before I could take a breath. I nodded gratefully.

"Who is he?" Zayana asked, her eyes widening at the sight of Retger.

"No time to explain," I said at the same time that Retger said, "Her brother."

He was already untethering the horses. "Who is here?"

"Wing Osprey," Zayana said. "He hunts us at the behest of Le Majest. He wants Aella."

Retger nodded sharply. "He won't be expecting three of us. Mount up. You can both ride Sesara."

I mounted the snorting black horse. He felt powerful beneath me, his muscles bunching and head tossing as Zayana climbed up behind me, wrapping her arms around me. Her breath came out in little nervous gusts.

"We ride," Retger said, making the sign of the bird, and then we were stepping out to the road, the horses' feet light and quick on the ground, their heads still tossing with excitement as they danced a little, eager to be off.

"I don't like this," Zayana whispered.

"Trust me. The horses are good ones or Retger would not have brought them. Our family breeds the best horses in Far Stones."

"That's not what I'm worried about."

But she didn't have time to clarify what she was worried about.

We reached the road and the horses leapt forward, moving from walking creatures to streaks of speed in the blink of an eye. I clung to the reins and the saddle of the horse I sat while Zayana clung to me.

"That's truly your brother?"

"Yes," I said.

"Has he been following us all this time?"

"Yes."

"I can't imagine that kind of loyalty." She paused for a moment. "He looks very strong."

"Hopefully strong enough," I muttered. But strength wouldn't be enough. Not with Osprey chasing us. Every moment that passed seemed to make the feather in my cuff hotter.

Morning streaked into a blur around us as the horses ate up ground so quickly that no one could possibly be able to catch up – not even Osprey and his glorious Os.

We'd ridden for maybe an hour when the light of the rising sun began to dim. I checked above us as I had a dozen times already. No silhouette in the sky. No sight of the purplish-white light of Os's wings. I didn't know why the light was fainter here.

Sesara danced under me, reading my mood. I felt edgy, waiting for the inevitable. Waiting for Osprey to descend on us. I was glad we hadn't had to face that yet – and yet part of me longed to see him again. And that was a problem.

By the time I saw him next, I needed a firm plan of action. Should I try to carve out the rest of that feather? Should I take any opportunity I could to kill him? If I didn't decide now, then I knew what I'd do. I'd stand there frozen in inaction because I'd hope that he was the Osprey from before the cathedral underground – the Osprey who wanted to help and to keep me safe. I shook my head, trying to clear the thought. Thinking about a young man who wanted me dead was a distraction I couldn't afford. I needed a plan and I needed to focus.

We turned a corner in the road, and I gasped.

Ahead, the road was completely enclosed by Forbidding. It curled over the dirt track, making it into a tunnel, continuing on either side, its dark tentacles clawing into the air, reaching for us.

"I've never seen it so close to a city!" Retger called from his horse. He was reining him in. I followed his lead.

We paused, our breath coming in quick huffs, as we watched the moving, breathing mass ahead. Retger drew his sword with care and I drew mine, too.

"You're sure you want to go to Ingvar, Shrikeling?" he asked.

"Yes." I forced every bit of confidence I had into my words.

"Then, we fight."

I kicked my horse up again and Retger kicked his up beside mine. We drew our horses neck and neck with practiced ease. Anyone who had ever ridden the roads in the north knew the drill. Two wide. Each of you was responsible for hacking your side of the Forbidding and keeping it from the other person. Retger had taken my left side on purpose, giving me the easier side to defend with my right-handed grip on the sword. We rode at a quick trot. Not so fast as to stumble, not so slow as to let the Forbidding slow us.

"I don't like this," Zayana said.

My wristband flared hotter and I looked over my shoulder as we reached the tangle of Forbidding. Was that a burst of purplish-white light on the horizon, or was my mind playing tricks on me? I didn't have time to wonder more. The first tentacle of Forbidding reached toward me and I deftly chopped it off with my short sword. It fell to the ground writhing as I moved to the next tentacle and the next.

I knew this routine. Control your breathing. Don't panic. Attack. Reassess. Attack again. I chopped and hacked at tentacle after tentacle, my grunts and labored breathing the only sign of my work. Beside me, Retger sounded the same as he cleared his side.

Our horses trotted further under the overarching boughs of dark magic, brave as only a Far Stones horse could be. Some people put blinders on them to keep the horses docile, but we didn't have to do that with Retger's mounts.

I risked a glance over my shoulder again. There was a last flash of light outside the tunnel and I could have sworn that I saw the briefest silhouette of someone removing a toothpick from his mouth. My heart felt a pang of regret for leaving him behind – which was crazy. I should not be thinking longingly of someone who was my enemy in action if not in spirit! – and then we were rushing deeper into the yawning mouth of the Forbidding and the muscles of my arm began to protest at the heavy work of fighting.

"We've lost whoever was following you," Retger said as the tunnel grew darker. "That's the good news. The bad news is that I think the Forbidding has closed over the mouth of the tunnel behind us."

I cursed.

The tunnel filled, suddenly, with scarlet light. Flame danced above Zayana's hand.

"Then it won't matter if Flame is visible," she said and she sounded relieved.

As an experiment, I let my bees free, too, and realized why she felt that way. The moment my manifestation was out again, I felt a sense of rightness. It was as if containing them swallowed a piece of myself. Maybe that was why Osprey had Os in view all the time. I wanted to keep my swarm visible, too – out where they could buzz in complete freedom.

"Welcome," I breathed to them. "You're always welcome."

I blinked, grateful for both the light and the feeling, but I didn't dare pause. I hacked at the next tentacle and the next, driving myself into a kind of trance as I worked.

I was so lost in the rhythm of it that I barely noticed when another view overlaid mine. A bobbing, similar rhythm. Only when I blinked myself to awareness, did I realize I was seeing through one of my bee's eyes and he was bobbing on a boat in the sea. Ixtap muttered something, turning his head and swatting at the bee, who only spiraled upward so he could look down at a ship packed with snake people. They looked odd on the sea, like an actual snake might if it flew. Odd, wrong, and horrifying on a bone-deep level. I shuddered and my vision flickered again.

Another bee was showing me another vision. It was a brief

glimpse, but I stumbled in my attack on the Forbidding, I was so distracted by it. Osprey leapt from his bird onto a thatched roof and quickly slid down the thatch, easing himself into the wide hay-door at the top of a barn. Inside, Wing Ivo was propped against a haystack, clutching his chest. Pain painted his face.

"I was too slow to catch them," Osprey said. "They have help now, too."

"Good," Ivo smiled as Osprey dug into a bag and brought him a flask and a tin mug. "I don't know why you're bringing me with you. I only slow you down and you know I won't help you find her."

"I couldn't leave you to die out there, old man." Osprey poured him a drink and held it out to him. "But I will have to leave you with a healer somewhere if we don't get that fever down."

"Don't leave me, boy," Ivo said, punctuating his words with a severe cough. "You know I can't abandon my Hatchlings. But you'll hear about this from the prince. That pact you two have – it was unwise to go against it. He torments you with it. He purposely pushes you to despair. He wants you to end the rivalry by your own hand – to end your own life. Surely, you must realize it. I knew it in the boat when he forced you to hold her head under. It would be better if you stopped searching for her."

Osprey ran his hand over his face, stress making his features taut. "Do you think I don't know that? I want nothing more than for her to escape me. If I could lend her my wings, I would. And yet, I am compelled to hunt."

"You should think about what you'll do when you catch her. She was never meant to be wed to a snake."

The growl in Osprey's throat was half anger and half pain.

I felt like I was leaning forward, wanting to know what was said next when my vision vanished. My eyes blinked open just as Retger leaned past me and swiped a Forbidding tentacle away.

"No daydreaming. Watch your half."

There were no more bee visions, only the steady attack and defense against the tangled Forbidding as the horses slowed to a walk. It was getting too thick to fight easily. My arms were getting heavy, my thighs rubbed raw from constantly shifting in the saddle to bend and swipe and hack. Even Retger was sweaty beside us, his face screwed in concentration. How far did we have to fight? No one could tell us. And somehow it made it worse to not know.

"Is it like this in the wild?" I asked him tightly. "Where our family is."

He glanced at Zayana, clearly not trusting her. "To a degree."

"You can trust Zayana," I said and he paused to give her a considering look at the same moment that her bird flared a brighter red.

A tentacle of Forbidding slashed toward him and Zayana startled, sending her bird toward it in a frantic squawk. My strike shot out, to deflect the attack before it hurt Flame. The strike was awkward, and I cursed as the tentacle slipped and bit into my hand.

"Come bees," I whispered. "I need your healing."

They were there in a moment, clustered around my hurt hand. The scent of honey filled the air and I felt instant relief.

I looked up and caught Retger staring.

"What?" I asked, irritably.

Zayana's laugh seemed to shake him back to himself in time to turn a new attack. "He's as horrified as we all are at watching you cover yourself in insects."

"As fascinated," my brother corrected her. "It's fascinating. It makes me wonder about the Forbidding. Is it a perversion of the magic that makes it possible to manifest birds and bees? Or is it some byproduct – some remnant left over from the production of those manifestations? Or is it some corrupt entity and at its heart is the source of all this rot?"

"Whatever it is, knowing won't help right now," Zayana said, but she had a considering look in her eye as she watched him and a faint smile. I hadn't seen her so happy since I met her. I nearly rolled my eyes.

"What? Never seen a red-eared Far Reach boy before, High'un?" Retger asked, noticing her glance.

"I haven't been missing much," she said with a sniff, but she didn't sound very sincere. She turned her attention to her bird and I almost fell from the saddle when it began to sing.

At first, Flame's voice was like any bird song. Bright, cheerful, filled with life. But as we fought back the tendrils of Forbidding, it morphed into something beyond a bird – into sounds like the choir I'd heard once on a trip to Vlaren. The song built, layer upon layer. The sound of viols and pandrums and a dozen more instruments coming together in a soaring theme, it built upon itself until it became the soul of a bird made sound.

My breath caught and I almost missed a Forbidding tentacle trying to pierce through to me. I recovered quickly, hacking it back.

"That's beautiful, Zayana," I breathed and even Retger looked impressed.

But he was more impressed a moment later when the tentacles closest to Flame curled back, giving him room to soar. And though we had to keep fighting off the Forbidding in front of us, the area around Zayana and Flame remained safe from the Forbidding. It pulled back to avoid the bright little bird and his enchanting song.

Now, that was a useful skill for a bird to have in the Far Stones.

"Are you sure that you haven't been here before?" Retger asked. "Because it seems like you have the kind of skills we could use around here."

Zayana said nothing but she seemed pleased with herself even though it was clearly an effort for her. Good for her. Her bird was worth more than she'd imagined at first. I bet those stupid Wings wouldn't be beating her for failure now!

My vision blurred for a moment and I was seeing with my bee again – this time, what I saw was Osprey, lifting Wing Ivo up onto Os's back. Ivo was pale-faced and he winced as he was lifted, leaning to the side to cough and cough until I was afraid he'd never catch his breath.

"I tracked her this far," Osprey was saying, in a low, miserable voice. "And it's only a matter of time before I find her. I wish you wouldn't suffer for it, old friend. You know I'll win and you know I can't help but persist in trying to find her. So … why not just let me leave you in a warm bed in an inn?"

Ivo locked his jaw and said nothing, and Osprey sighed.

"You won't be able to stop me from catching her and you are only slowing me down by a few hours. Is a few hours of freedom worth so high a price?"

"You tell me. What would you give to have two hours free of your binding to Juste?"

Osprey's face was so pale it almost looked green, but he shook his head as he hopped onto Os's back beside the Wing, reaching down to steady him carefully. They sailed up into the air and my view jittered as my bee followed in fits and starts and a nausea-inducing ricochet course up through the clouds. From up here, I could see a city surrounded by darkness – a creeping, living darkness crawling its way toward that bright coastal city. That city could only be Glorious Ingvar. My eyes really hadn't been lying to me. He'd tracked us this far. Being able to fly had given him a powerful advantage that even the undertrails couldn't mitigate.

I blinked back to my body and found myself sprawled on the earth, my head ringing and pain in my side. Retger was yelling something from above me. I could tell by his labored voice and grunts that he was fighting as he spoke. Zayana's voice was nervous. The horses screamed and her voice became even more anxious. But I couldn't make out the words. The singing of Flame was too loud as her bird did his part to shrink back our adversary.

"Aella? Are you with us again?" Retger spared a glance down at me, his blacksmith's muscles bulging as he shoved back against the Forbidding.

"Yes," I said thickly, grabbing my ringing head in both hands.

"I'll get you out of this mess as quickly as I can," Retger said. "Hold on."

I felt for my short sword but it was gone. Spinning in place, I searched for it and was nearly trampled by my horse when I reached across the ground. It was only Zayana's scream that warned me. Everything seemed thick and hard to hold onto.

There was something I needed to tell them. Something

important. I tried to think of what it was, but my feet slipped and the ground came up and met me with a crack to the chin.

CHAPTER NINE

"Easy! Easy now!" I woke to the sound of Retger quieting the horses. "Can you wake her? We need to move!"

"Aella?" Zayana called.

I nodded my head. "He's hunting us. He's close."

"The Forbidding will stop him," Zayana assured me, helping me to my feet.

"Who is hunting you?" Retger asked. "This Osprey guy? Tell me about him."

"Osprey is the Wing assigned to the guardianship of Le Majest," Zayana said reverently but she looked at Retger like she was weighing his reaction to her words and when he made a sour face at what she said, she frowned. "He is bound to hunt down and kill anyone who threatens the life of Le Majest."

"And let me guess, Aella did just that?" My brother sounded amused.

"Yes. She's openly defiant. She insists that the freedom of her family is worth dying for. I've tried to tell her it's crazy. But she's stubborn and she never listens." Zayana's eyes were wide as she pled with Retger to be on her side.

"I'm right here." I pulled myself to my feet again and Retger handed me my sword. He was on foot and so was Zayana.

"Maybe you should talk about how stubborn I am when I'm not right in front of you."

"Surely now that she has family here, you can show her a better way," Zayana said. "I saw a narrow dark cloud pass behind a white fluffy cloud before I went to sleep last night. That should mean the protection of a greater, purer force. She needs your protection."

Retger nodded, keeping a straight face even though I could feel a smirk lurking behind his stony look. We were all crowded together, Zayana's bird holding back the Forbidding as she lectured him.

Zayana's words turned urgent. "When we leave here, he will fall on us immediately, but if she goes with him and does as she is told, there will be honor and she will live."

"I thought you agreed to be on my side!" I objected.

"I want what's best for you," Zayana looked pious. "Surely your bother can see that. He will help to guide you. What price should you pay for a freedom you'll never have? It's not worth your life!"

"What is freedom worth, then?" Retger asked Zayana.

"Freedom can't buy safety or happiness. It can only buy you troubles and hardship."

Retger turned to me. "And is freedom worth trouble and hardship to you, Shrikeling?"

I bared my teeth. "Let them try to take it from me and I will show them what it's worth."

Now, he did smile. "I hate to disappoint you, High'un, but I am one of heart with my sister. I'll gladly give my own life to carve out a little freedom for my family. Even if that Wing is waiting on the other side of the Forbidding, I will still stand with her and fight."

"Good," I said, feeling my cheeks heat. "Because he is waiting there."

Retger drew in a breath, a look of surprised irritation on his face.

"But I have a plan. I'm sick of being the prey. I want to be the predator."

"Fine words, Shrikeling, but freedom is not so easy to gain."

"I have an idea," I said with an answering grin. Well, maybe not a plan, but it was the beginning of one. "But I'm going to need your help. And we need to make it work before we can leave this tangle of Forbidding."

"He won't be able to bring reinforcements into this place." Retger nodded approvingly. "A good place to kill a Wing. If he escapes our grasp, then the Forbidding will get him."

"You seem very calm about the Forbidding," Zayana said, crossing her delicate arms over her chest. She was different around my brother. She had more of a spark of life. Her eyes constantly sought his as if he was the rock he looked like and she could tie herself to him.

"I'm used to it. I've been fighting it all my life, just like Shrikeling here, but I've been doing it for longer." Retger's grin was confident.

Zayana nodded, her cheeks flushing slightly.

"Have you ever caught birds in traps before?" I asked Retger, interrupting them. They could save all their getting-to-know-you for when this was done.

"Sure," he agreed. "A pair of eagles for the old man when they were stealing foals."

"Is there a good way to do it?" I asked. "Because this might be a man who is hunting us, but he's as much a bird of prey as he is a man."

Retger nodded. "Okay, we travel until we're almost out of this stuff and then you two will have to hold back the Forbidding while I make the trap. But I won't do it unless you're both fully committed to it."

He looked at Zayana, raised an eyebrow, and her eyes widened.

"If you think it's the wisest course," she said demurely. That wasn't an eyelash flutter, was it?

"I'm your big puffy cloud, aren't I?" he asked. "Hide behind me."

Zayana's chin lifted a hair more and she was smiling as she mounted her horse again.

"Thank you, Retger," I said quietly.

He grabbed my arm, looking furtively at Zayana before whispering in my ear. "When we have some privacy, I have a lot to tell you that isn't for idle ears. Things about our family and our connection to the Single Wing. Okay? You would have been told after you failed to Hatch like the rest of us were but … well, that didn't happen, right? Just know that we have allies and that once we get to Ingvar there will be people to help us find this general of yours."

I opened my mouth and then shut it with a click. They all

knew? And they hadn't told me? But I knew better than to ask in front of Zayana. She still wasn't sure where she stood, and I didn't want her to have any information she didn't need to have until she was committed to our cause. Especially when it came to the safety of our family.

I mounted up in front of Zayana just in time to take a swipe at an arm of the Forbidding tangling toward her.

"If we stayed on foot, Flame could keep them off of all of us," Zayana said. Flame's song was still strong, though I was growing used to it enough that I was no longer marveling at the beauty and just focusing on the utility of it.

"We need to ride," Retger said. "Before we all grow tired in this mess. Why don't you give your bird a break? We're going to need it for my trap."

"Him," Zayana corrected him. "We'll need him."

I ignored their dance of words and focused on my bees for a moment.

"Light our way," I whispered to them. That wouldn't take much energy and Retger was right. Zayana should rest Flame's ability until we needed it.

Her scarlet bird winked out of existence and we were swathed in the dull golden glow of my swarm of bees. Almost immediately, the attack of the Forbidding redoubled, and Retger and I had to put all of our concentration into fighting our way each step through the tangle. It was almost as if a bubble surrounded us, a bubble of malevolent tangles and reaching tentacles.

"Can we set fire to it?" Zayana asked after what felt like hours of fighting.

"Not without finding the heart," Retger answered her. He bent around her protectively as he slashed away an attacking tentacle. "In a tainted tree or a Forbidding bear, it's easy enough to find but this is basically like the wilds of the Forbidding. It's impossible to find a heart to light on fire."

"Forbidding bear? That sounds awful!"

"They're rare. I doubt we'll see one."

I wished he hadn't said that. Somehow it felt like if the worst of something could happen to us then it would happen.

"What if you found the heart of the wild Forbidding? Could you light that on fire?" she pressed.

She sat stiffly, awkwardly, behind me as if she felt uncomfortable that she couldn't fight, too. I was dripping with sweat, my cloak too heavy and clothing too hot, but I didn't dare remove it. These days, I seemed to lose anything not attached to me.

"It's something I hope to do someday," he said with a conviction that surprised me. I turned to study his face. He'd never talked about that before. "It has to be out there somewhere. This stuff isn't completely mindless like a plant, but it doesn't seem to have individual consciousness like an animal. It's smart enough to attack but easily outwitted – like right now when we're surrounded by the stuff but can still fight it back. That suggests there's a mind or heart of some kind for all of it. But where to find it? And would you have to fight like this to drive it back?"

"I wonder if all of Glorious Ingvar is surrounded like this," I spoke my fears aloud. "How do they feed their people?"

"They probably ship food in through the port." Retger shrugged. "It was surrounded like this once before. The people can fight it back again."

"Without swords?" I pressed.

He looked away awkwardly. But that was why we were fighting like this. I almost sagged with relief when we finally saw a glimmer of daylight on the other end. We fought until it was a wide tunnel. I could see the outlines of the city in the bright light beyond. It was nearly sunset. We'd been fighting this back all day. No wonder my whole body ached.

"We set the trap here," Retger said after a minute. "He'll be expecting Aella and Zayana but not me. So. We set up Zayana here." He pointed to a spot on the side of the road near the Forbidding. Absently, he hacked off two tentacles as he spoke. "You'll need to hold the horses and have Flame keep the Forbidding off of you and Aella while we wait."

"If you say so." She sounded nervous. Flame sprang to life on her palm and then hovered above us, beginning to sing.

"I was planning to make a net with my bees," I said, crossing my arms. "Nothing you have can hold him."

"You need to be the bait," he insisted. "In bird traps, you use live bait. Usually, a smaller bird. So, we'll use a Shrike."

He winked and I nodded. He wasn't wrong. Osprey would be coming for me, not Zayana. I was the bait, but this wasn't how I'd hoped it would go down.

"Your net idea is good," he said. "You can use it to grab his magic bird. I don't have anything for that."

"And Os is very strong."

"You have a nickname for him?" Retger looked worried.

"That's the name of the bird. The osprey. It's called Os."

"Oh, okay. You handle Os with your bees. You'll be lying on the ground looking injured, so you can squint to see. We'll lay out the saddlebags behind you and I will lie wrapped in a cloak there. When he drops on you, I will grab him with a noose – just like a big bird."

I chewed my lip. It wasn't the plan I'd had but it wasn't a bad plan. I was just worried about the bees and Os. My bees were amazing – no doubt about that. But Os was huge and powerful. Could they really form a net around him?

"Look," Retger said. "It doesn't matter if your net thing doesn't work very well. The key is to distract the magic bird. Once I have the noose around your pursuer's neck, he'll stop whatever magic he's doing. He won't have a choice."

I nodded my agreement. I was trying not to think about what we'd do after that. Trying not to think about how we were supposed to drag a prisoner along with us into a city. Those worries could come after we'd accomplished this. I wasn't going to kill Osprey. I knew that much. Whatever else we had to do, it wouldn't be that.

"No mortal wounds," I said.

"I'll do what I have to do, Shrikeling. No one hunts down my sister to be the bride of anyone. In Far Stones, our family is free."

Zayana watched us clasp hands with something in her eyes that looked a bit like longing.

"Give me your horses," she said arrogantly and then gasped as Retger handed her his reins. "No. We shouldn't do this."

"Why not? Worried I'll get hurt?" Retger asked with a teasing grin.

"You crossed your left rein over the right when you handed them to me. That is inauspicious in the extreme." She made the sign of the bird, worriedly.

"How does she know these things?" Retger asked me.

I shrugged. "Apparently, we're all supposed to know them."

I was already lifting the saddle bags off the horses for our ruse.

"Tell me more about how you think we can destroy this Forbidding," Zayana was asking Retger but I was too busy worrying to listen. No one knew how to destroy the Forbidding. Not Retger. Not anyone. Or we would have done it already. Even the Hissan would have done it. I knew their minds enough to know that.

No, the Forbidding was just one more obstacle to our freedom from the Winged Empire. That had to be our goal. It was a great goal – one that was even worth risking Osprey for. Or at least, that's what I was trying to tell myself as I called my bees to me in a small swarm. It was growing harder to deny that thinking of hurting him hurt me.

I could still feel his forehead pressed against mine. I could still feel his pain as he watched me with agonized eyes the moments before I stabbed him. I could still feel the desperation dripping off of him. I felt in the cuff, felt the growing heat of the feather within, and let myself feel – if only for a moment – the mixed emotions I had about him. I was excited to see him again. I shouldn't be. I was meant to be trapping him.

And yet, my heart was racing at the thought of seeing those bright eyes and that toothpick dancing across his curving lips. I was also terrified to see him. Because it would mean pain. His or mine. It was always pain. I'd run for days and taken terrible risks to flee him, and yet it often felt like we were tied together somehow. Like I could feel him on the other end of the tether and if he wasn't chasing me, then I would be chasing him.

I shook my head. It was girlish emotions like these that would seal my fate. Even if he felt the same way – and I didn't think he did after he denied me that kiss – even if he felt attraction to me, he would still obey every command of Le Majest. He would beat me and carve me up and serve me up to his prince as a tattered bride. Even if it ate him bite by bite to do it, he would. Caring about him was like walking into the ocean and taking step after step even as the water closed over your head. I shouldn't do it. And I was already being swept away.

I tried to shake away my thoughts. If Retger had any idea I was thinking like this he wouldn't just scoff. He'd take me by the scruff of the neck and shake me. I'd have to keep these thoughts to myself.

I called my bees closer. I needed to do this before I reconsidered. Their buzz was muted, almost as if they were as uncertain as I was.

"Work as one swarm," I whispered to them. "You are mighty together. You are strong. You are not alone, you are part of the greater swarm that stretches toward the skies. You know that even your death is small compared to the greatness of your swarm that stretches through the ages. So, your story does not end with you. Your glory and bright light does not end in you. It is in your swarm, in your togetherness. Take courage and take risks. Work to do the impossible. You will be a net of hindrance around Os when he leaps from the sky. You will tighten together around his wings. You will hold him fast. You will not fear his strength or his fury. You will not be overcome by him. Because you are mine and I will give you my heart and my courage to keep you strong."

I could only hope the invocation was strong enough.

I lay down dutifully on the ground, letting my bees lie with me – a trap waiting to spring.

CHAPTER TEN

He descended on us. Death from above. A flurry of flapping wings and blinding bright purplish-white light. It was good that my role was to play dead because I couldn't have done anything else, I was so stunned by his arrival. It wasn't that I wasn't expecting it. It was that it was utterly gorgeous.

One moment, I was lying on the ground, eyes squeezed shut, hoping beyond hope that this would work. The next moment, he was there, riding his Osprey through the tunnel of Forbidding in a snarling crouch. His short swords were in each hand and he fought – double-handed – against the Forbidding as he swooped between snatching, clawing strands of it. One strand fell at the sweep of his blade, writhing on the ground, only to be met by another and another.

I'd barely managed to catch my breath and squeeze my eyes shut as he descended on me, leaping from Os's back, his words gusting over me. "Dead or alive, you're mine."

Something in my chest leapt at those words. It wanted to throw itself into his arms, wanted to make those words true. I wanted to open my eyes and see his face as he said them.

The rest of me stuck to the plan.

"Net," I whispered, reminding my bees. "Be strong now!"

My eyes snapped open, meeting his, and the wonder on his

face swept all thought away. He was here to capture me, and yet the look on his face as of absolute reverence.

The bees surrounded Os, leaping up from their cloud into carefully regimented squares to form strands of net around him, a buzzing swarm of stinging fury. He screeched and Osprey spun away from me to lend his help at the same moment that Retger leapt from behind the horses, flinging his noose toward Osprey's neck.

Osprey's blue eyes lit with fury and he sliced the rope as it passed, bisecting the noose easily. How had he seen it in time? It had been over his head!

My heart lurched in my chest as I launched myself to my feet. This wasn't going according to plan!

I clenched my fists and bees manifested to cover them.

"You think to trap me?" Osprey took a step toward Retger. "Who are you?"

He looked both shocked and furious. He made a swift hand gesture and Os bulged with purple light. He swelled to nearly double the size and I gasped as my bee net burst into a hundred little individual bees. They spun toward me, stunned and off-balance, knocking into everything around them as they tried to reform a swarm.

"To me, bees," I gasped. Off to the side, Retger was drawing his sword now that his noose maneuver hadn't worked.

No. Not a good idea.

Everything in me revolted at the thought of my brother going up against my … whatever Osprey was. One of them would kill the other right before me and then what would I do? I couldn't bear it.

Gasping with fear, I lunged, hands spread wide, bees flowing from them toward Osprey. I wanted them to form another net – this time around him.

Instead, his eyes went wide, and he reached through the golden stinging mass, gripped me by the forearms, and sang a single note. In the blink of an eye, Os was under us, bursting upward. We shot through the air like a star across the night's sky. We shattered the Forbidding tangles above us and broke into the sky.

Osprey's eyes were wide, his hands shaking as he held my arms.

"House Apidae," he gasped, as if he couldn't believe he was holding me. His touch was almost tender, as if he was afraid to hurt me. He wrenched one of his hands loose, reached in his pocket, and shoved something into the pocket of my jacket.

"To buy wisdom," he said.

"Will you take me back to your master?" I asked, breathless.

"What choice have I?"

"I'll find you one."

My bees hurried to join us as we spiraled upward, a swirl of purplish-white feathers and furious golden bees. A buzz filled my chest as a memory of his song rang through my mind. I grabbed the opening of his half-buttoned jacket with my freed hand and his eyes widened further, his lips parting and eyes melting as if he thought I was going to kiss him again.

But my other hand was already moving. And my belt knife was in it. I ripped his shirt open and plunged the belt knife into the blood-soaked bandage wrapping his chest – just to the left of the stain. Hoping, beyond hope, that I could hit the second half of the feather.

"I'll cut you free."

As the knife met his flesh, pain ripped through my heart. Stabbing him felt like stabbing myself. My lips fell open as I tried to pull in a frantic breath.

I looked up at his eyes then, terrified at what I might see. They were hot and thick with emotion and the corners of his mouth turned up into what could almost be a smile.

"Though you slay me, yet will I rise," he said, eyelashes fluttering. His grip on my shoulders loosened as his body went slack.

With a cry, I dropped my belt knife, wrapping my arms around him.

His osprey vanished and we plunged through the air for a single heartbeat and then his eyes flickered open and the bird reappeared, settling under us.

Something firmed in his gaze and he reached for me, but I'd lost my knife. I didn't dare risk what he might do next.

"We all do things we hate to make it possible for what we love," I whispered, throwing his words back at him, and then I leapt backward, falling through the air.

I spun into a dive, hoping to be faster than Os. He must be slower with Osprey hurt.

"Catch me. Catch me," I chanted to my bees.

They formed up under me in a cloud, slowing me as I tumbled to the tear in the Forbidding that we'd made on our way up – and then through it and to the hard ground below. It was enough to keep me from breaking my neck, but not enough to keep from jarring every bone in my body.

"Nnngh." My pained groan filled my ears as hands tugged me up.

"What now? What do we do now?" Zayana sounded panicked.

"We flee! And next time we set a better trap." Retger grunted as he lifted me to the back of his horse. I was still blinking stars from my eyes as he leapt into the saddle and kicked his horse into a gallop, Zayana's horse straining right behind. "Come on, Welaro, run! Run as the wind sweeps over the hills!"

The horse galloped at a breakneck speed and we left the last shreds of Forbidding behind us as we sped into the sunset toward the spires of Glorious Ingvar.

Behind me, I heard a roar of anguish.

Osprey.

The same anguish ripped through my heart. What had I done? What had I done?

I looked back, but I couldn't see him. I could only feel the steady throb of the hot feather in the band on my wrist.

As we raced to flee him, I kept seeing that melted look in his eyes as he parted his lips. It replayed itself over and over in my mind. By the time we reached the gates of Glorious Ingvar, our horses slick with sweat and huffing, I thought the memory might consume me.

CHAPTER ELEVEN

"He's better than I thought he'd be. Quicker," Retger said irritably. "So are you. Those bees are something useful. In nature, it's the smallest things that usually have the biggest bites."

I made a sound of agreement in my throat, but my mind was elsewhere. I kept feeling that tug toward Osprey. Twice, I almost leapt from the back of the horse to run back to him. I shook my head, trying to clear it. He would be okay. I knew he would be. But wasn't it strange that the bee I'd set to watch Juste was watching Osprey instead?

At the thought of Juste's name, I felt something like rage simmering in my belly – and another tug. This time to the north and east. I felt my jaw dropping open. I could feel him. I could feel where he was if I really tried to. It was the honeycomb in Juste's belly – I was sure of it. It had bound me to Juste Montpetit in ways I didn't want to be bound and it had also left this thread between us. I shivered. If I could feel it, perhaps he could feel it, too.

"He'll be after us again," I whispered. "He'll be better at it next time."

"So will we," Retger assured me grimly as he led us through the gates.

"Ho, Traveler!" the gate guard called, stopping us with an outstretched polearm. "All arrivals must register at the gate and if you know of a path through the Forbidding, you are required to list it."

"List it?" Retger asked, dismounting, and taking the pen and writing in the ledger thrust at him. I moved nervously in the saddle. There would be no keeping this record from Osprey. He had to know we'd be there, but I hated leaving more evidence. Hopefully, Retger was being circumspect in what he wrote.

In my mind's eye, I could see Osprey arriving and checking the ledger for my name. I felt a thrill of anticipation at the thought of it. He would follow, and next time, I would be ready.

"House Bald Eagle is organizing a push to clear the road," the guard said. "Any information we can gather will help them. How did you make your way through the Forbidding on the road? Was there already a clear path?"

"We carved our way," Retger said, flashing a dimpled smile. "Like all good Far citizens."

"Just the three of you?" the guard looked suspicious. His Claw uniform was immaculate, and his sword handle bright and polished. He likely wasn't from these parts.

"I'm worth ten men when it comes to fighting the Forbidding," Retger said with a wink, finishing his work on the ledger. He'd better be careful with bragging like that, or they might recruit him.

The Claw nodded to him. "You're free to pass, citizen."

He took back the ledger and we stepped through the walls and into Glorious Ingvar. It was all I could do to keep my mouth shut and my worries to myself as Retger led us through the packed, winding streets of the city. Hawkers were closing their shops and taverns lighting the lamps over their doors as sunset sank into darkness. The scents of the city – mouthwatering bread, the fecundity of horse dung in the streets, the sharp tang of sweat, and the ferment near the tavern – filled my nose and made me feel like just one person lost in a sea of life.

The city was large. I lost track of where we were in the winding streets before we'd taken more than a turn or two. They were not laid out straight or in a grid of any kind. Rather, it seemed that buildings had been erected on any empty space and the spots between them were packed dirt merely because they were there to walk on, not because anyone had thought through whether it would be a good design for the city.

Thankfully, Retger seemed to know where he was going. He stayed on foot, leading our horses, his eyes alert and his steps firm.

"Have you been here before?" I asked, but I knew he couldn't have been. I knew all the places he'd been and he'd hardly been out of Far Reach more than I had.

"No."

"But you know where we're going?"

"Yes." He turned and shot me a firm look – a clear order to keep my mouth shut, but I didn't know why. Was there some secret to how he was navigating? I narrowed my eyes and tried to guess what it might be.

Eventually, he found his way to a tall, narrow building. The stables were on the ground floor and a huge sign hanging over them proclaimed this was the Kingfisher Inn. It rose three more stories above the stables and ended in a peaked roof.

Retger had a quiet word with a tough-looking man with one eye who stood watching from the door of the stables. Coins exchanged hands, and then the horses were being taken and we were dismounting and following Retger up a narrow staircase that opened up to a wide common room.

In the room, there was a long bar with smaller tables filling the rest of the room. My head was still spinning from the hurry of our ascent and I barely took in the chaos of the room. Someone was playing a viol, people were dancing and eating, and the conversation was so loud I couldn't hear Zayana when she tried to whisper something to me. If this was what cities were like, they could count me out!

Retger leaned over the bar and spoke to the bartender who turned, took a pair of keys off the wall, and handed them to Retger with a bored expression on his face.

I barely had time to open my mouth, never mind object, before Retger was sweeping us up the next flight of stairs and down a hall to where two tiny rooms stood side by side. They were numbered. He opened the first, glanced at the narrow single bed and washstand, and then opened the second and handed me the key. It was identical to the first, but there were two narrow cots in it.

"Your accommodations, ladies," he said with a grin. "The barkeep says there are baths at the end of the hall."

"Then I'll be going there immediately," Zayana said primly, taking the key from my hand, but I didn't miss the way her eyes stayed on Retger until she absolutely had to tear them away, or the way he seemed to subtly flex his muscles as if aware of her scrutiny. It was all I could do to keep from rolling my eyes. Seriously? We were a bit busy fleeing for our lives, or hadn't they noticed? It was like watching a mating dance between a pair of birds in the spring.

Retger motioned to me and we ducked into his room together.

"Finally, a moment to talk," he said, but he looked awkward as he said it, chewing his lip. Emotional moments had never been his strong suit – but that was true of my whole family.

"How did you find your way through the city?" I asked.

"The Single Wing leaves signs. Little scratch marks that tell you the way to safe houses or friendly inns. They're at the bottom of the corner of the buildings. I followed the marks."

"Oh," I said, feeling foolish. Everyone knew things I didn't. "Can you teach me?"

"Sure, but not tonight. They're complicated."

I nodded. "He'll be able to follow them, too. Osprey. He's also of the Single Wing."

Retger nodded, considering. "And yet he hunts you for Le Majest?"

Why did I feel so defensive about that? "He's bound by magic."

"We'll have to move quickly, then. We'll go to find these records at dawn." He double-checked the closed the door as if he was afraid of people listening in and then continued in a low voice "I told you we had things to discuss. About the Single Wing. Look, the old man used to take us aside after the Hatching ceremony – after we didn't Hatch – and he'd tell us. He would have told you that night if … well, he wasn't there to tell Alect or Raquella either. Abghar told them instead."

I felt a pang at his words and blinked back tears. I missed them all. Having Retger here was like a taste of home, but it couldn't be enough.

"When Father arrived on the beaches of Far Stones with the other settlers – this was before our mother arrived and they married – there were things that were done to clear the land. Things that were unspeakable."

"They used blood to drive back the Forbidding," I confirmed. So. Juste had not lied about that.

Retger looked uncomfortable. How much had my father told him about what happened then?

"Among other things. And sometimes when they fought the Forbidding, they said there were men within it. But they did not reason with these men, they slew them on orders from Le Majest."

"The crown prince?"

He shook his head. "He wasn't even born then. The Emperor. He gave orders that anything found within the Forbidding was to be killed or burned. The settlers did that and they carved for us a land and a home. But in their hearts, horror and shame were born. They hid any ruins or signs of life that they could – not bridges obviously, but anything else. They didn't want to think about what they'd done." That explained why the entrances to the undertrails had been disguised. "And it made their bonds to the Empire of War and Wings chafe. And that was when the Single Wing was born. They marked themselves and swore to one day take this land for themselves and drive out the Empire as they had driven out the Forbidding."

"They didn't do a very good job," I said, glancing out the tiny window. "It's back."

"No battle is ever fought just once," Retger said darkly. "Anything you have that's worth something has to be defended and bought again and again and sometimes the price is steeper than you could have hoped. The old man paid with his life. We might, too. But freedom is one of those things that's worth fighting for again and again. No price is too high."

I swallowed as I thought of my father. "Are you sure about that?"

"As sure as I am of anything, Shrikeling. At any rate, the old man joined the Single Wing with the rest of them, and when we come of age, we join, too. We're all in it. Every one of us. The in-laws, too. And that's why I can help you here because I know who to talk to and who can help us. I have connections and I know the signs. We'll find your information here one way or another. I'm going to go out and I'll find where those records you need are from the times of the settlement and then we'll go look at them together."

"I should be the one finding them," I protested.

He was already shaking his head. "When your pursuer comes, he'll be looking for you. He didn't see much of me – likely not enough to describe me accurately. So, I should be the one to go into public. Do you have any coin?"

"A few," I said, fishing into my pocket and pulling out the coppers Wing Ivo had given me.

"Buy yourself dinner down below," he said. "We'll try to resupply tomorrow. And promise me you won't leave the inn until I return."

"I'm not a child, Retger. This is my responsibility."

"Look, is it really so bad to have a bath and a meal and catch some sleep?" I was going to keep arguing with him but then his eyes narrowed. "How well did you know that Wing? The one who is hunting you? That look in his eye when he saw you wasn't what I expected."

"We're friends," I said, a little too quickly.

"Friends who hunt each other for the Empire?"

"It's complicated." My arms crossed over my chest of their own will.

"Friends who look longingly at each other like they're about to speak binding vows and leave married?"

I rolled my eyes. "Come on, Retger."

"Just stay in the inn." He was shaking his head, all brotherly protectiveness and worry. He shoved me out the door before I could protest and locked it behind me. "Baths are that way."

And then he was gone, leaving me frustrated and – yes – in need of a bath. By the time I found the bathing area, Zayana was gone and the attendant was pouring a fresh hot bath. She left as soon as it was full, and I took the opportunity to sink into the hot water. That alone nearly put me to sleep. I hadn't bathed properly in … not since I'd left home. I even attempted to wash my long curls, surprised to find little bits of twigs and leaves stuck in the mass of hair.

Eventually, the water went cold and I had to leave the warmth and dress again in the soiled clothing from the road. I cleaned the jacket and hung it on a hook in our room to dry. There was no sign of Zayana. Maybe she was eating. I tried not to worry but I'd gotten used to having her around.

I sat on the edge of the bed – just for a moment. I'd get food in a minute. I just needed to sit to rest my bones. I didn't even realize I was nodding off until I awoke, sprawled across the cot. Zayana was snoring in the other cot, but when I glanced out the window, the moon still showed it was early in the night.

And I was hungry. I grabbed my freshly cleaned jacket and headed below.

CHAPTER TWELVE

The common room was still buzzing with people. I ordered dinner and a drink from a girl serving tables and then found myself a spot at an unoccupied table. The common room had owls carved on every bit of wood. Owls in flight. Owls peering out of holes in trees. Owls on tree branches. It was oddly comforting.

I was just sitting down when my vision flashed to my bee. It was the one with my family.

Raquella's worried face flashed across my vision. "It looks like people lived here. Recently. Those are carrots on that table."

"Just clear it of debris," Abghar said, exhaustion thick in his tone. "It's the only place with four walls that we've seen in days. We'll sleep here tonight."

"And the owners of the house?"

He shook his head at the same moment that my vision flickered back. The serving girl was putting down my dinner in front of me.

"Thank you," I said wanly. The stew smelled amazingly good. I ripped into the bread and began to chew when another vision hit me. When I was tired, they seemed to come more often.

It was Ixtap again, screaming from the bow of a boat. Spray from the surf kicked up and across the bow, spattering him. He seemed unaffected, simply raising the bright torch he held in his hand and calling out an order.

"Command the adders to swim more swiftly! Seasonal winds may be against us, but valor is with us!"

Could snakes actually swim? I shivered and the vision disappeared. Gratefully, I dipped into my stew, only realizing after I'd begun to chew that someone was sitting at my table.

"It doesn't do to eat alone," the young man sitting opposite from me said. He wore a red coat, much like mine, only his was embroidered in thick black thread with a design of kestrels. "I'm Shanigar of House Kestrel."

"How nice for you," I said, taking another bite of stew. I did not want company. I wanted to eat.

His smile turned a little cold, but he kept talking. "You could use the company – especially if you are traveling alone. Le Majest has sent to the main continent for reinforcements, but it will take time for them to get here and until then, we all must be patient."

"What do we need reinforcements for?" The rich beef of the stew coated my tongue so that I was hardly even listening to the smiling man. He was in his early twenties, his hair slick and light in color while his skin was dark. It made me think of Osprey's skin when I'd plunged my dagger into his chest. Had that really only been hours ago? I shivered.

My hand started to twitch as the memory filled me and the man took it.

"You're not from here, are you? You look an awful lot like the description says you will."

I tried to jerk my hand away, my other hand searching for my belt knife. But it was gone. I'd lost it when I stabbed Osprey in the chest.

The man reached into his jacket.

"I wouldn't," I squeaked out, my hand still pinned in his grasp, but then I lost all sense of what was happening to me as the vision crashed across my sight.

It was Osprey. Of course, it was. It was always Osprey now.

He was on his knees beside a campfire. I could see Glorious Ingvar in the distance, down the hill. It shone with a thousand tiny lights like someone had planted a field of candles. Beside the fire, Ivo sat, coughing into a handkerchief. He could hardly seem to catch his breath.

"Let me help you," Ivo said grimly. "You don't need to soldier through this, too."

That was when I realized that Osprey had his face in his hands. He looked up and I realized his eyes were glazed over and his cheeks were tracked with tears. He wasn't wearing a shirt. He began to unwind the ruined bandage around his chest. My more recent stab had left its own bloody stain beside the original one.

"She sure is a stabby one, that Hatched of mine," Ivo said, coughing again.

"My hands are tied, my friend." The sorrow in Osprey's voice was a heavy thing. And the wounds on his body – some bandaged and some scabbed over or opened again from our fight – were everywhere. Each one was a reminder that he'd hurt himself to keep me from pain. "And my heart is tied to something else. I thought I was strong enough for this. I thought I'd hardened myself to the point where I could no longer break, but I am breaking." His whole body shuddered. "I'm tearing in half. Every day brings me new agonies. I'm set on a path that I can't turn from. I have to see it through or break in the process."

His eyes came up and met Ivo's compassionate gaze, his lips falling open as fresh tears tracked soundlessly down his cheeks.

"He's doing it on purpose," Ivo warned. "You should have hidden your heart better. Now he knows what you want, and he will take it from you if only to make you break your vow, break the bond, and hand him everything. You're the only one with any chance of curtailing him and he knows that. He's no fool, Osprey. He'll fight with every weapon he can grab. And she is a weapon against you."

"There's no way to prevent that, now."

The last winding of bandage fell from his chest and I felt myself gasp. Half the feather was gone, yes, and my knife had pierced the other half, but the skin where the feather had been cut out had turned a mottled red and black – inflamed and swelling around the wound and seeping badly. Spider-leg streaks of red shot out from it across his chest and up his neck. My "help" had been no help at all.

"What happens if the feather is completely cut out?" Ivo asked.

Osprey shook his head. "I think she thinks it will break my bonds."

"And will it?" His words were tense.

"I think it might just break me."

The vision faded and I cursed. I wanted to see more. I needed to know more. The fool holding my hand had it in an iron grip now.

"You are her." There was a glitter in his eye that told me I was in danger. "You're a wanted woman. The price on your head is high enough to –"

I didn't let him finish the sentence. I sprang to my feet, ignoring the stabbing agony in my torso. He expected me to pull away, so he yanked me towards him, around the table. Which suited me perfectly. I spun in toward him, snatching my short sword from where it was hidden under my cloak. Without breaking his grip, I let him pull me close and ended my spin with the edge of the sword under his jaw, tip nicking his sensitive throat.

"Enough to make you think twice about being a fool?" I asked.

He swallowed and the bobbing of his throat brought his flesh down enough to nick it on the blade.

"Release your grip," I said calmly.

He let go of my hand.

"And be on your way." I clenched my jaw hard after I spoke. I didn't want to let him go. I was so angry these days – so furious at a whole world that wanted to take advantage of me – that all I wanted to do was jam that knife up into his throat and end the threat right there. I hated the thought of this strange man waiting in the shadows. I hated the thought of him pouncing the moment I turned my back.

He jammed a parchment against me, his hands shaking.

"I won't be the only one," he said, looking around the inn. "Did you hear me? There's a price on her head."

It was only then that I remembered that the glow of the dancing fire and the smell of beef stew and fresh bread weren't the only things in the inn. The dozens of people filling the common room were there, too, and they were all standing, staring at the two of us.

"And she has a weapon!" he spat. "She violates the orders Le Majest made to keep our community safe."

The crowd watching us remained owlishly silent.

"But it's not very safe, is it?" I said quietly. "Outside the city gates the Forbidding slips toward this city, bent on swallowing you whole. And here in this inn, I am bent on your destruction now that you've told me you're my enemy. So, you tell me. Is it safe?"

"No," he said, the sword tip nicking his throat again. He flinched at the bite.

"Maybe you'd like to leave while you can."

"Yes."

I withdrew the sword just long enough to watch him flee the inn. Around me, everyone remained still as his footsteps echoed out the door. I leaned down and picked up the parchment he'd dropped.

It said:

Empire of War and Wings Imperial Order

Detain Alive and Unharmed

Female, seventeen years, bushy dark hair, brown eyes, Far Reach accent, traveling with weapon, violent in nature. Watch for bees.

Reward – Fifteen golden crowns.

Well, wasn't that nice? There was a reward on my head. And I doubted that those coming to collect it would remember the part about detaining me unharmed. Le Majest would end up with a dead bride for his troubles – which would suit me better than being a living bride. Angry, I threw the parchment on the table and drove the place setting knife through it.

"Did someone else want to collect?" I asked the room, chin lifted high.

There was silence, and then someone laughed. I spun, eyes narrowed, to see the innkeeper grinning nastily.

"This inn belongs to the Single Wing," he said. "We don't bow to Emperors or their get."

At that, a roar of agreement rose around me, surprising me, and then one man stepped out from the crowd. He had a lantern jaw and fiery eyes.

"Three of you traveled here together. And from what I see, you're solidly with us. You should get some rest and get ready. Tomorrow, we fight."

"Fight what?" I asked, surprised, as I sheathed my weapon.

He looked proud as he spoke, "We fight for our freedom. Tomorrow, at dawn."

"But the rest of the continent isn't organized," I objected. This was a bad idea.

He shook his head. "And they never will be. The Forbidding is at our doorstep and the pigeons flew today telling us Le Majest sails here and will arrive the day after tomorrow. If we don't fight now, our chance will be lost. If you need more weapons, talk to Gill at the stable door. We riot at dawn."

A chill swept over me, but I nodded grimly, not sure what else to do. I could feel their eyes on me, feel them watching every move. One slip, and I'd be in worse trouble than any imperial order could put me, worse trouble than any single man in an inn common room, worse trouble than I could make for myself – maybe.

So, carefully, I smiled, pulled the knife from the warrant, and made the sign of the bird to them with it. There was another cheer and I drank down the rest of my drink as they returned to their conversations.

Carefully, I finished my stew, snatched up the paper, and concentrated on keeping my manner casual as I strode from the common room and up the stairs. I needed Retger. And we needed to get out of here. Now. Before we were dragged into a war in the streets we hadn't asked for and couldn't win.

Fear lit my every step, seeming to spike as I knocked on Retger's door. There was no answer. I slid into my room and saw Zayana was still asleep. No help there. Frustrated, I sat down outside Retger's door and leaned back. I'd just have to wait for him here.

I reached into my pocket and was surprised to find something there. Wait. Osprey had shoved something in my pocket, hadn't he? Why would he have done that?

I pulled it out, inspecting it in the lantern light of the hallway. It was a standard-sized silver coin, though the stamping was different than I was used to. Usually, all coins bore the Swan on one side and the face of one of Les Majest on the other – the Emperor, or the crown prince. This one had the crown prince's profile on one side. Which was usual, though now that profile made me shudder, bringing back memories of swaying snakes and threats of my tongue being cut out. The other side was the surprising one. It was stamped with two heads facing opposite directions. Two identical faces, looking out from the center. Where their heads met at the back, someone had merged them together, topping both with a spiky crown and wreathing the whole coin in stylized wings.

The two brothers. I knew the story.

Generations ago, two brothers had inherited the kingdom when their father – the Emperor – died. They were born twins, and the midwife – in a way that added drama to the legend – had mistakenly forgotten to record which was born first, and so none had known which was the heir. They accepted the crown together. Two rulers. One kingdom. Coins had been stamped and feasts had been held and then – predictably – greed and power had overwhelmed them, and they had carved up the Winged Empire between them and gone to war. The war had lasted three years, and it only ended with one man's head on a pike.

Since then, when Le Majest inherited the crown, he had his siblings executed. "Refining the blood" was what they called it.

This coin was some kind of commemoration of that time. Though why anyone wanted to remember it, was a mystery to me. I spun it round and round, staring at the two faces. Why had Osprey given me this coin? A silver was valuable. It could keep me fed in this inn for a week. And yet, I hardly thought he'd been worried about my room and board when he'd jammed it into my pocket as we flew through the air. Was it a message of some kind? And if it was, what could it possibly mean?

I put the coin back in my pocket and tried to think, but I was worn from our journey. My thoughts blurred as the minutes ticked by and eventually, exhaustion stole me away and I fell into a fitful sleep, leaning against the door.

Elsewhere in the Winged Empire…

Wing Mirala watched her bird as it made wide circles over the small patrol ship. When her gull wheeled like that, screaming in the sky in pleasure, she wished she could fly, too. Even the searing joy of riding the waves from peak to peak on the fast skimmer was nothing compared to the heights of the spirit bird. The way it soared and dipped, skimming over the spray, was elation come alive. But while the gull could lend Mirala her eyes, she was not large enough to be ridden as some manifestations were.

Mirala still daydreamed about riding her, though. Rushing through the clouds in a burst of wings and feathers and searing joy. She closed her eyes over the daydream, letting it settle into her heart for a moment and warm her spirit as it always did.

So close to Kestrel City, there was nothing of concern here. The Winged Empire had dominated these waters for four generations without a single attack from without or rebellion from within. Patrol duty had become nothing but a routine pleasure she could soak in. The sea. The sun. The wind. Bliss.

Her gull screamed and her eyes popped open.

She let them unfocus so that she could see with the gull's eyes.

What in the …

She blinked twice, hardly believing what her manifestation was showing her from its place high up in the sky.

A fleet. A fleet bigger than anything Mirala had ever seen – bigger than the Fleet of the Garbocco Islands, bigger than the Terns stationed in all their glory in the harbors of Kestrel City.

Her breath caught in her throat. She needed to report them

and get the small patrol ship out of the way before that mass of ships swept through these seas. But the Tern Captain would want to know who had sent a fleet against the Winged Empire. He'd want more information than she had right now.

She needed to get her gull closer to see.

Her eyes tightened in concentration and her gull swooped toward the ships. She channeled courage into the bird. There was no sign of any other spirit birds over these new ships, just Kiralala and her pinkish-white spirit wings like the faint glow of disappearing dawn. No reason to fear. Kiralala was quick and could dodge any arrow launched from a ship. She would be safe up here scouting.

Mirala studied the ships, looking for a flag or a sign – any way to tell where they had come from. They were built strangely as if they had been grown from twisting vines rather than constructed of wood. Sails that rippled silver in the light seemed almost like fish skin – patterned and flashing in the sun.

She shook her head, confused, and then the captain was there.

"Wing Mirala? Does your bird see something?"

She hesitated, not sure how to report this as her bird swept in close for a better look.

"Wing Mirala?"

No flags. No markings. So strange.

Her bird swept in closer, searching, searching.

Men and women in masks and foreign clothing scrambled across the deck of the nearest ship and then one of them raised her hands.

A snake as thick as Mirala's torso shot from her hands into the air, snatching Kiralala from the embrace of the wind and dragging her down to the ship.

Mirala couldn't stop the scream that bubbled from her throat any more than she could stop the snake as it wrapped around her spirit bird.

"Wing Mirala, what is happening? Where is your bird?" The captain sounded frantic. He should be frantic.

She opened her mouth to warn him and then the snake squeezed around her bird, so tight, so chokingly tight.

Her eyes went wide as her life fled with her bird's.

BOOK TWO: BATTLE FOR THE HEART

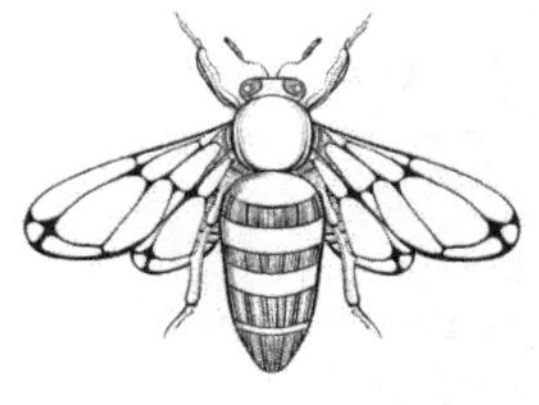

We keep what we catch.

Stories and souls.

Dreams and Sight.

Come in and Fetch.

Hearts and tales.

Hopes so bright.

Open with Blood,

Pay our price.

Bind your eyes.

Lose what you Loved,

Empty and cold.

It all grows old.

Lay bare your Desire,

Great or small,

Gain it twice.

Burn on our Pyre

Bright and hot,

Soul made naught.

- Ancient Poem from before the Founding

CHAPTER THIRTEEN

I awoke to noise below and pounding footsteps. I was still blinking myself awake when Retger turned the corner at a sprint, skidding across the rough-hewn boards of the inn floor.

"We have to hurry!"

"Where were you?" I asked but he shook his head. He had a fresh cut in his scalp, and it was bleeding. I struggled to my feet, catching his arm as he fumbled for his key. "Retger! Tell me what happened."

He flung open his door and snatched up his pack. "I didn't have time to get your new clothes or anything. I found my friend in the city and he told me the old records are in the Oriole Monastery in the west end of town. They have a library in the monastery but it's a bit of a trick to get in. Then, he took me to a group of the Single Wing and there were debates that led to arguments that led to violence."

His breath came out in frustrated huffs.

"They want to attack today," I agreed. "They plan to riot."

"Plan to?" he scoffed. "They already are! And your description is all over the city. You're wanted by Le Majest. Alive."

I nodded. "Which means we need to hurry."

"Find Zayana. We'll leave the horses here. The streets are too packed for horses right now."

I paused in the entranceway. "Will they be safe?"

"Find her!" His eyes were wild, more fearful than I'd ever seen them. I didn't ask anything else. I ran to the next door and opened it in a burst to find Zayana cross-legged on her bed, Flame hovering over her. She paused mid-song, her eyebrow raised.

"Zayana," I gasped, "we have to go. Now. Retger knows where. And there's trouble."

"There's always trouble where you are, Aella. It's those bees. They aren't happy unless they're stirred up."

There was no point arguing. She wasn't wrong. Since the moment I'd heard a buzz in my head, my life had been a maelstrom of trouble.

I ran out the door and nearly collided with Retger.

"Ready? Let's go."

He didn't wait for us to respond. He hustled down the hall in the other direction from the stairs, took a sharp turn, and opened another door. He was all business, his eyes flashing and his actions tight and economical.

A gust of fresh air hit me in the face and I realized this was an outside staircase leading down to the ground. Retger was already out the door, his feet flying down the steps. I followed, but not as quickly. I used this chance of looking from so high up to scan the city. What I saw shocked me. Spirals of smoke rose up into the sky, lit with spiky red flames from multiple places in the city. The roar of voices – their words indistinguishable – met my ears and every glimpse of roads showed bodies huddled together, hands held high. I couldn't see faces from here – but I could still feel the energy of the crowd like it was a wind in my face. It roared over me, sweeping away my confidence in its frustration and hatred. It was like my own emotions had been amplified and mirrored in these crowds and looking at it dead in the face, filled me with fear – fear for what they might do and fear for what I might do. Suddenly, I understood Retger's panicked eyes and speeding footsteps. I hurried until my own feet felt like they might take flight.

"Retger! Which way is it to the monastery?"

"It's west. In the far west district of the city near the Oriole Fountain."

I had no idea where the fountain was, but it would be a landmark to watch for.

He grabbed me by the arm – Zayana, too – and leaned in close. "Stay together. Stay near buildings if you can so the crowds don't sweep you away. If we get split up, we'll meet back here at the inn, okay? It should be safe." He glanced at it. "Maybe you should stay here anyway, Zay."

Since when had he given Zayana a nickname?

"I want to come with you," she said determinedly.

He nodded, adjusting his brown curls so that his headband held them back better. "No manifestations. They draw eyes. Especially since the order for your detainment mentions bees, Aella." He nodded his head as if trying to convince himself of something. "Stick with me and it will be okay."

He flashed us a confident grin that I didn't believe for a second and then we hurried from the alley where the stairs exited and out into the main street.

I was nearly knocked over the moment we stepped on the

street. Sound hit us hard – a babble of chanting voices and a clash of metal from up the street. I looked toward the clash and caught a glimpse of blue jackets embroidered in white – Imperial Claws. A rock hurtled through the air toward them but before I could see it land, Retger was pulling me in the other direction down the packed street against the tide of bodies. Fury filled every face and in the hands of most, ordinary tools were brandished like weapons. Shovels and cleavers, pitchforks, and meat hooks. I felt a chill run down my spine at the look of the makeshift weapons – somehow more ominous than simple swords and hunting knives would be. It reminded me too much of the day I'd Hatched and what happened afterward.

"Eyes to yourself!" Retger hissed as he pulled us farther with him. The press of the crowd was getting stronger. They shoved and pushed as they tried to enter the fray. It was quieter as we moved away from the open conflict, but the quiet here was a quiet of anticipation – the quiet of the wolf before it leaps, of the pit before you fall into it. It stole my breath away with the undercurrent of rage and violence just waiting to spring out and attack.

I wanted what they wanted. I wanted it just as badly. But this was all wrong. The wrong way to do it. The dumb way to do it. It should be organized and planned, not this fomenting free-for-all.

We reached a square and I could tell by the way Retger was eyeing the other side that we needed to cross it, but it was packed with people.

Something smashed. A bottle, perhaps.

There was a long scream in the background and a burst of light overhead. I glanced up to see a bright seagull spirit bird swoop from overhead. It sank into the crowd, snatching someone up in his talons. He soared upward and dropped the man, letting him fall into the crowd as screams lifted into the air. He was already wheeling to do it again.

We'd been heading west into the square, but now, in the very direction we wanted to go, the people were being driven forward by a double line of Claws and a pair of Wings with grim expressions. The spirit seagull dove again, snatching someone new from the crowd. While a second seagull plunged into the crowd beside me and grabbed the face of a man of about forty. His clothing was well-made and his beard oiled. The scythe in his hands dropped first, as he clawed at the bird and then the screams started. The bird was trying to lift him up by the face, its spirit wings glowing an ominous sunset red. The wings flapped, spirit feathers spiraling away, bright and choppy looking. He was too heavy for the size of the bird, but though he fought, it kept him pinned in place, his feet just inches from the ground. And then the man went limp and the bird dropped him.

My gaze shot to the Wings. One of them swayed – a wrinkled man with a grim face – but he quickly recovered his balance and the bird shot out again.

"We need to get out of the square!" I warned.

Retger nodded, trying to work his way south, but the crowd had the same idea and we were caught up in the rush of bodies as they pulled us with them. I could barely catch my breath, barely even see faces as we were pushed and squeezed and battered. Pain flared in various places – knee, shoulder, gut. I clung to Retger's hand like a lifeline. My hand was growing clammy as we tried to make our way southwest across the tide of people headed south.

I caught Zayana's eye and her lips compressed grimly. People – I realized – were looking at her. Noticing her court dress, worn and frayed as it was. Noticing her Imperial features and long sleek hair. She did not have the look of a Far Stones girl, hacking her living from the Forbidding and the rock. She carried herself with grace like she was always dancing and kept her chin high like she was balancing a jar always on the crown of her head. And right now, that wasn't good.

"Hunch!" I called to her.

But she shook her head, confused.

"Retger!" I called over the constant wall of sound. "Retger, look at Zayana."

He met my eye, puzzled, and then looked over at her. His face lit with understanding at the same moment that I heard a whispered, "High'un" from someone nearby.

The word echoed, bouncing from one set of lips to another.

Zayana shrank closer to Retger and he pulled her in tight with one arm, releasing my hand to draw his hidden short sword with the other. His eyes were narrowed and deadly, a few curls escaping the leather thong around his forehead. He was ready to strike.

I watched the tip of his short sword with worry. In this crowd, it almost kissed the backs of those in front of him. One wrong stumble, one twisted step, and someone could be skewered.

"High'un" was echoing again and now "sword."

The pressure around me seemed to increase as more bodies pushed me against Retger. I could feel the emotion of the crowd in the air like the greasy feeling before a lightning strike. Anxiety and violence hung over them like a fog. My hand itched for my own sword and it was all I could do not to draw it.

There was a roar behind us and a new clash.

I glanced over my shoulder and froze as a pillar of flame burst up into the air from the square where we'd been only minutes before. Someone shoved me from the side, and I stumbled, falling to one knee. I scrambled up again, hearing my name called.

"Aella?"

But before I found my feet, I was shoved again. I clawed up, tugging at my cloak. Someone was standing on it. My vision was filled with snatches of people and things as I was pushed and shoved, knocked and jostled. I tugged again, more desperate, and suddenly my cloak was free.

Straightening, I looked for Retger and Zayana. Gone. They were gone. I spun, looking, and saw them. Somehow in stumbling, I'd been pushed toward the west side of the street while the crowd had propelled them to the south.

I caught Zayana's eyes and saw her try to point to me, but Retger was tensed, sword tip pointing a pair of men who were screaming in his face. I tried to move along the wall of the stone building toward them, but someone hit me from behind and my face smashed against the stone.

I took another step, wiping blood from my crushed nose, holding Zayana's gaze for one more minute, and then my vision was lost as my bees poured their news into my mind.

Not now!

But I had no control over it. An image seared across my mind. Alect fighting the Forbidding. Raquella was down. He slashed the darkness above her head, reaching for her. She screamed and the tentacles of Forbidding wrapped around her.

"No!" he screamed at the same moment that my own mind screamed the word. But she was gone.

His sword was fast and sure as he struck and struck against the tangle. My breath caught as I watched, hoping, believing he could do it. There was an arm! He cleared another tentacle away, but a new one snatched for him and it was all he could do to sever it.

"Please," I begged. "Please."

He launched himself at the mass around her, wrestling with them with blade and sheer will power.

And then it was gone and my vision returned only to realize I'd been pressed into an alley by the flow of people. I was halfway down it, pushed along by a less dense crowd here. I turned, meaning to run back to the street where Retger and Zayana were, but strong hands grabbed my arm.

"Not back to the street, girl, there's fire there!" an older man said.

I glanced behind us and saw he was right. Dark smoke billowed behind us.

"My brother," I gasped.

"The alley comes out on Colonization Road. It runs parallel to Chigger Way. You can follow it south and find him there," the man said hurriedly as we scrambled down the alley, chased by smoke and screams.

I gasped and choked, unable to take a breath, my mind still struggling to comprehend what I'd just seen. Had Raquella been killed? Or would Alect get to her in time? Anxiety left bitterness in my mouth at the thought.

I followed the older man, hoping he was right, but when we reached the next street, it was obvious I'd never make it south to the next alley.

CHAPTER FOURTEEN

The way was blocked by a double line of Claws. So close as I was to their advance, I could see the citizenry attacking, lobbing rocks the size of my fist or chunks of masonry. Screams filled the air along with battle cries as the Claws stabbed and hacked, never stopping in their march forward, even as they left a slick of blood and fallen bodies in their wake.

I tensed as I tried to decide what to do. I could join the fight – though that seemed crazy. Just because I agreed with the rebels didn't mean I thought this would work. If I'd learned nothing else from Karkatua, I'd learned how quickly the innocent were swept up with the guilty in a house-to-house fight in the city and I would never choose to risk children like this.

I could return to the inn like Retger had suggested. Likely, he and Zayana were already fighting their way back there to meet up with me. Which meant they'd have a stronghold to stay safe in – no matter what I chose to do.

Given the way this fighting was going, any library was at risk. There were already fires. Out of the corner of my eye, I saw a group of men swinging a long bench at the barred door of a brewery. Who knew if the monastery would still be standing after today? And that meant getting there and finding the information that would lead me to the general had to be the top priority.

The street was maybe four cart-lengths wide. The crowd was less dense here as people either fled the Claws or attacked and were mowed under the churn of their feet. If I chose to cross, and if I wasn't fast, I'd be rolled under, too.

I took a big breath and darted across the street, dodging projectiles and furious bodies as they smashed forward into the Claws. The rebels wore no uniforms and had nothing in common except for the same fury that filled every set of eyes. A fury I shared.

A cry of "Freedom!" pierced the air and "War and Wings!" followed, but I kept my gaze forward, my heart thundering in my chest like a galloping horse. Why hadn't we brought the horses? Even though they were slower, they would have given us an advantage. My breath was raw in my throat. I skidded on the slick cobbles and had to leap over a fallen huddle that had once been a man.

I was mid-leap when the vision hit. I tried to push it away. It did not budge. Instead, I willed my feet to keep running even as my vision was snatched away and my mind went to where my bee hovered over the shoulder of Osprey.

He was cursing. Loudly.

Below him, Os glowed his steady purplish-white. Ivo was crouched on the bird in front of Osprey. His harpy eagle – golden and strong but not strong enough to carry him – flew beside Os and a little behind him.

Osprey and Ivo were bent down, eyes tracking the ground as they circled the city.

"They sprang too soon," Ivo was saying, an aching sound to his words. "Haven't they been listening? The other cities aren't ready yet. We have no real leader, no general for the militia we've been raising. No way to win this. They'll be slaughtered."

"And we'll lose a key city," Osprey said as Os banked, circling Glorious Ingvar. From here, it was easy to trace patterns in the streets below. Walls of blue met with ragged lines of figures throwing projectiles or attacking in ones or twos. Lines of bright orange fire snaked down streets as they leapt from building to building. Smoke curled up and then was snatched by the wind and pulled inland. It looked as if a hand had raked itself through the smoke as one might rake soil.

And then the wide, yawning blue sea met my eyes – choppy and raging as it smashed itself against the rocks. Small ships bobbed in the cerulean waves beside white flecked foam. Some were in a scatter pattern, spreading out from the city, but one long line of ships sailed toward Glorious Ingvar.

"There. He comes," Osprey said, pointing to the ships. "Faster than I could have wished. And meanwhile, she's down there somewhere in that tumult."

"You're sure of that?" Ivo asked. "Perhaps they skirted the city. Perhaps she was too smart to go into the city, knowing you'd be looking for her there."

"They didn't." Osprey jammed a toothpick between his teeth, his lip twisting upward as he studied the ships in the distance.

"If you hadn't found them in the Forbidding outside the walls, I would never have guessed they could make it this far so fast." Ivo shook his head.

"You doubt me?"

They turned the corner of Os's circle and started to fly over the west side of the city again. I caught a glimpse of something below them – a bronze fountain. An oriole! I tried to see more, but my bee jittered too much to get a good view of the streets surrounding it.

"Of course not. I merely wonder how it was done. I do think you're obsessed with her."

"I've been forced to obsess over her. You know that."

Ivo coughed, long and harsh, but it didn't change his worried look. "It's not just that."

"We talked about this last night. There's only one way to end this that I can tolerate, but not before I'm certain she has a chance."

My vision returned to my body, like the snapping of a string and I gasped.

I was slumped against a wall, my clothing wet and clinging to me. I'd made it across the street – which was nearly empty now except for the slumped bodies of those hacked down by the Claws. Here and there, a blue-jacketed body joined the heaps of civilians, but the death was mostly on one side – the side of the citizenry. They must have left me for dead, too.

The clash of weapons and shouts of orders could still be heard with the marching of boots as they continued up the street, heading north.

I struggled to my feet, shivering in horror when I realized my clothing was wet with blood – and not my own. I caught a glimpse of something down the street. More blue jackets. Reinforcements.

Swallowing down bile, I darted into the nearest alley headed west. I didn't dare get caught by the second sweep of Claws. This time, they might stab me to make sure I was dead.

The alley was empty except for discarded items and things broken in the passing of so many feet. I scrambled along it, my feet shaky under me. I was worried about Retger and Zayana. And my wristband was burning hot again. But I was committed now to finding the Oriole fountain and the library in the monastery before it burned or was smashed to pieces.

I stumbled over another body and I turned to the side, vomited, and then kept running.

I just had to press on and not lose my head.

Relentless, Aella. Be relentless.

The alley came out to a winding street littered with debris. Two buildings were on fire here. One had a sign with a grinning pig and a cleaver – a butcher, obviously – and the other had a pair of carts sticking out of the open side. A city carter. Two people who would lose everything they owned. And what would they do tomorrow when their businesses were in ash and their families destitute? Most people in cities lived above their businesses – like a miniature homestead in a densely populated place. With no coin for food and no roof over their heads, the very first night would be a bad one, and every night after would only get worse. You couldn't start over with no supplies, no food, no clothing – with not even a weapon to carve your way through the Forbidding. They'd be smashed into poverty in the blink of an eye.

Had the rioters even thought of that when they lit these buildings on fire? Was that poor sprawling corpse in front of the butcher's shop the owner of the place?

I shook my head to dislodge these thoughts. But it didn't work. I could imagine building a place like this – hour by hour, day by day, spending the chunks of time that made up a life to build a business. All that life-time invested was gone now. If the owners still lived, then their years had been plundered. Almost better to be beaten than to have that taken. At least you could recover from being beaten in a few weeks. You could never recover these years. And you'd have to spend those hours all over again to build it back.

I hurried down the street, huddling against the buildings to avoid the roar and rush of the flames. My skin tingled painfully at the heat as I hurried along.

Shouts and cries filled the air as neighbors scrambled to pull their things out of homes and businesses before the flames spread, or to toss water on the roaring inferno. It all felt like not enough. A hundred people fighting these fires would not be enough. And this was just one fire on one street. I looked up at the sky and my heart felt sick. The smoke gathering above the city spoke of dozens of fires just like this.

My eyes stung with the smoke and I clenched my jaw and pushed west. There was a square here. Good, maybe there would be a street heading directly west. I pushed out into the square and gasped.

Every way out was blocked by overturned carts and furniture. People scrambled to push them in place, blocking the paths to the west and south. I hurried through the square toward the west barricade but just as I reached it, someone grabbed my arm.

"That's a pretty jacket you're wearing, girl. Red. Embroidered. Draws the eye."

It was a young man about my age, face streaked in soot and sweat, but not bad looking. The leather strap around his head held back longish wheat-colored hair and his upturned nose had a playful tilt to it, but his eyes were hard.

"It wouldn't fit you," I said shortly, pulling my arm from his grasp.

"It doesn't fit you, either. At least, not if you want to live in our streets."

"I'm just passing through," I said shortly, plunging toward the barricade.

A man's head popped over the tangle of carts and broken furniture. His voice was laden with anger when he spoke.

"No one passes into our street without our say so. We stand for the people."

"Great," I said shortly. I was running out of time. "I'm one of the people. Let me through."

The boy my age grabbed my arm again, pulling my jacket up around the wrist. "Don't see a Wing here. Do you love the Empire of War and Wings, girl? Are you one of their pretty little playthings?"

I had my short sword out in a flash and against his ribs. I was feeling very stabby.

"Playing at revolutionary, are you?" I hissed. "Playing at standing up to the Winged Empire with your broken furniture and lighting your neighbors' shops on fire? Does it make you feel like a man?"

His face darkened and I realized that the street had gone quiet, all eyes on me.

Forbidding take it!

"What are you doing in our neighborhood?" He shifted his weight as if to indicate that he was changing the direction of the conversation.

I could try a lie, but what was the point?

"While you fools light your own city on fire and get your own people killed," I said through gritted teeth, "I'm busy working for the real revolution and we need information from a monastery in this city. I was on my way to get it when you all went off and decided to have your little mock-revolution ahead of time."

"Ahead of time?" he growled. "This has been years in the making."

"Yes," I said coolly. "Imagine the horror the real revolutionaries are feeling right now as they watch you burn their carefully laid plans in the ashes of your city."

His face paled but he let go of my arm.

"Where are you headed?" the man from behind the barricade asked.

"The Oriole Fountain west of here," I said.

"You can pass," he said grudgingly. I hurried to scramble over the tangle of wood before the boy could stop me. To my surprise, he followed me.

"You're going to need help getting there," he said.

"I can manage myself." I kept my words curt. The last thing I wanted was someone tagging along. Someone I didn't know. Someone I didn't trust. Someone with a hot head.

He whistled – long and piercing – and there was a flurry of sounds – the noise of multiple people moving clumsily. I glanced around me and had to clench my jaw to keep from cursing. Three other boys my age hurried toward us, gripping impromptu weapons – kitchen knives, the leg of a chair, a fire poker. Their awkward grins told me they weren't attackers. This was getting worse.

"I don't need anyone coming with me."

"You said we weren't starting a revolution the right way," the original boy said, "so maybe if we follow you, we can change that."

"Let me be clear," I said shortly, hurrying now that I'd made it over the barricade and into the busy street ahead of me. People here hadn't seen the scourge of fire or Claws yet. They were busy boarding up doors and windows and barricading their street. I saw buckets of water being lined up along the street in case of fire. Someone here had a little common sense, at least. "I don't want anyone coming with me. You'll get yourself killed."

"We can handle ourselves," my unwanted companion said, his chest swelling out as he spoke. "I'm Oman. Of House Whiskeyjack."

"Good for you." I bit my words off. "But people around me die. Messily. You should stay here and help fill buckets. Make yourselves useful."

"You're a real revolutionary, aren't you?" Oman said, undeterred. "Even though you don't have a wing on your wrist."

"Not all of the Single Wing have their tattoo on their wrist," I corrected. I didn't even know why I was bothering to respond, but I couldn't help but fight him on that detail. In my mind's eye, I was seeing a single wing tattooed behind an ear. A very nicely formed ear. I felt my cheeks growing hot. "But I don't have a tattoo anywhere."

He nodded sharply. "Sometimes we need to hide who we are

so we can strike at the right time."

I shot him a sideways glance wondering at his sudden seriousness, but it immediately faded into a puppy-dog grin again.

I sighed. "Please, all of you go back."

We were nearly at the barricade that had been erected at the other end of the street. I needed to lose these boys here in this safe place before they all got slaughtered because of me – and drew the attention of the Claws at the same time. I was not recruiting a militia. I was just trying to go read an old book.

They didn't even respond. They just formed up around me like they thought they were my Claw escort.

"Please." Now I was begging. "I don't want to watch you all die."

"Death is better than being beaten into the ground day after day by the Winged Empire." Oman said and for the first time since he started talking, he sounded sincere.

And there was no denying it, so I stopped pleading with him and saved my breath for running. I'd just have to try to slip away from them on a busier street.

I reached the next barricade and vaulted over it, into the horrors beyond.

CHAPTER FIFTEEN

The barricades had been a little oasis of peace in the middle of a war. The moment I reached the next street, the oasis was gone. People ran in schools like fish, clutching possessions, or supporting the injured, their eyes wild and faces drawn. They looked often over their shoulders as screams ripped through the air to the north and south of the street. I couldn't make out enough to know who was screaming or what was happening, but I knew that I couldn't stop any of it. It was like a moving ship on the high seas – no anchor could bring us back to peace.

We plunged westward.

I kept my eyes focused on where I was going, dodging people and barriers as they came. I didn't dare let myself feel what the people were feeling or think about their situation. I didn't dare imagine what might happen to this city in the hours and days to come. Every time I slipped and my mind went there, my heart plummeted. I must only focus on what was ahead of me.

My vision began to darken.

No! Not now! Forbidding take it!

And then I was lost in the vision again. I was hovering just over Osprey's shoulder. He was on the street. A Claw's fist shot out, about to hit a woman in the side of the face. She wasn't even looking. Osprey's hand shot out lightning-fast and caught the fist in his grip, his muscles bulging as he shoved the Claw back a pace.

"Enough!" he roared. "Peace, you fools! These are citizens!"

But no one was listening. Beside him, Ivo coughed, doubling over, but his arm was held out sword brandished as he swung in defense of an elderly couple stumbling by. He stood toe to toe with my pursuer, attempting to help Osprey quell the conflict. They were situated squarely between a line of Claws and a line of citizens, arms up, faces grim as they tried to hold them in place.

It took me a moment to realize they were at the port side of the city. Behind them, a row of ships' boats was bobbing over the waves as they hurried toward the city from the ships anchored further out. The wind was against them, but the men in the boats pulled on their oars with vigor.

"Enough!" Osprey roared again and his bird smashed in between the two lines of enemies, flaring in purplish-white light. I was blinded for a moment and when I blinked my vision back, I was seeing through my own eyes again, panting as I tried to regain my balance.

The boys on either side of me had shoulders under my arms, dragging me – stumbling – through the street. I could hear the march of feet behind us.

"Hurry, revolutionary girl," Oman whispered. "They're almost upon us. You had some kind of fit."

They pulled me with them into the doorway to a building – a bakery, I thought. It was recessed, leaving just enough room for the four of us to huddle together in the shadows.

"They came out of nowhere," he said in hushed tones. "So fast. All we had to warn us were the screams."

"Shhh!" one of the other boys said – a lanky fellow with a kitchen knife and hair so long that even his forehead band couldn't keep it out of his eyes.

We shrank deeper into the shadow at the same time that we heard the Claws issuing orders and the screams of citizens as they were hacked down by the line of marching Claws. They were getting closer. They were on our street.

Fear seized my heart. I wanted to draw my short sword, but even that would be too loud right now. I clung to the grip, hands growing clammy as the marching steps drew closer and closer. They stopped outside our alcove and my breath hitched in my throat. I could see the merest glimmer of blue and white from my vantage point. The edge of a uniform.

A roar of voices filled the air.

A bottle crashed on the cobbles in front of us, igniting immediately with flames.

"No quarter!" the Claw outside our hiding space roared.

There was an answering roar from down the street.

"Prepare to hold the line! Hedgehog formation!" the Claw officer's voice boomed.

The other roar was getting closer. They were going to clash just outside our hiding space. My breath was coming so fast I couldn't slow it. Someone deeper in our shadows whimpered. I didn't blame him.

The sounds of feet pounding on cobbles grew louder and louder and then we saw them – faces matching in grim determination were their only uniform but they pounded forward, makeshift weapons raised. Some of these rebels even brandished real weapons. They roared with one wordless voice, throwing themselves into the fray.

My breath caught in my throat at the horrific sounds that followed.

"Forward. One. Pace!" the Claw officer ordered, and the ground seemed to shudder under their boots as they stepped into my full sight, flinging adversaries before them in their steady, cut, jab, step, cut, jab, step.

A second wave of rebels smashed against the solid rock of the Claws washing across their shield formation like a wave on the rocks. One of them fell headlong into our alcove, clutching his throat, coughing and hacking on his own blood. Oman reached down to help him, and I caught the rebel's wide eyes as they glazed over. A second rebel stumbled in, eyes wide, mouth a rictus of pain. He slashed out with a homemade polearm and one of the boys with me screamed.

Like lightning striking, the end of the Claw line spun and lunged, three of them reaching into our alcove. They grabbed Oman and two of the others by their shirts, ripping them out of the alcove. I drew my short sword, hot on their heels, but I wasn't fast enough.

The first boy went down, throat slashed open in a wicked line. He didn't have time to scream. The second was run through at the same moment that I leapt from the alcove. I barely got my sword up in time to deflect the strike at Oman's chest. It rattled awkwardly off my defense, sending a shudder up my right arm so that I almost dropped the weapon. I gasped, thrusting my left hand out and manifesting my bees.

The Claw in front of me screamed as they swarmed him, and I reached down and tugged Oman up. His teeth chattered as he tried to speak.

"Run, you fool," I breathed, barely managing to pull him along as the bees distracted the attacking Claws. They wouldn't hold them for long. I knew that much. Their stings were too mild, and they had no other weapon.

The last boy fled the alcove – the one with the long hair and the kitchen knife.

"Dahn," Oman said through chattering teeth as the boy threw an arm under him and began to drag him along the buildings behind the Claws and back the way we came.

If the Claws weren't busy fighting the line of rebels, they would have already turned and slashed us to pieces, but they were busy at their work – efficiently shredding one human after another as they marched down the street.

Only the ones who had confronted us in the alcove seemed to notice we had escaped.

"There was an alley back there," Dahn said with a grunt. He was struggling under Oman's weight.

"Walk, Oman," I hissed, grabbing his other arm and helping to drag him. He seemed to shake himself and find his feet just as it looked like Dahn might stumble to the ground.

Two of the Claws detached from the group, starting after us.

We dodged into the alley just as I heard a stern order call the Claws back. But we weren't safe here.

"You boys need to run home," I said breathlessly.

"Those were bees!" Oman gasped. "Bees! You're … are you a Wing?"

"No," I growled, sticking my head back around the corner.

The Claws had stopped their march forward. The officer was speaking with one of the ones who'd fought us. My bees were hurrying back to me, and he pointed at the cloud of them as they fled. Forbidding take it!

"We don't have time for this. You need to go!"

"You don't know the city," Oman said breathlessly. "And we do. You need us."

"You're going to die if you stay with me. Just like your friends did." I hated being so blunt. Hated how it made it sound like their friends didn't count. But that was the thing. They did count. And so did these two. I didn't want them all dead because of me.

"Reed and Farlo are already … dead." Dahn stumbled over the word, face pale. "We can't change that. Come on."

I followed him – but mostly because it was the only way we could go. Down the alley and deeper into the city. Always deeper.

Before the first turn, we heard boots on cobbles following us. We ran as fast as our lungs could stand.

CHAPTER SIXTEEN

Minutes faded into hours in a steady grind of flee and hide.

"If we were walking straight there, it would have taken an hour," the boys kept saying. But it was poor comfort when every turn saw our route blocked again by sword or fire or screams. It was impossible to say who was winning in the maelstrom of the city. All we knew is that it wasn't us.

We were coated in soot and grime, throats burning from running so often. We'd caught a drink in a fountain, but we hadn't even drunk our fill before that square was filled with fighting and we'd had to run again.

"Almost there, almost there," Dahn was breathing from our spot huddled against the door of a dye merchant.

His chest heaved with every gasp. He'd lost the kitchen knife hours ago and he held his left arm close to his chest. I was pretty sure he'd broken it when he fell in that same encounter. The Claw chasing us had scraped his back with snatching fingers. We'd barely escaped – wouldn't have except for a shoal of rebels who filled the square at just that minute, launching rocks from slings at us. It had been enough to buy our escape – but Oman had been clipped in the back of the head with one of the stones and blood still flowed steadily from the wound. I didn't like how his eyes kept going out of focus.

They were adamant about staying with me.

"Bees," was all they said when I tried to convince them to go. "Never seen bees before."

Perhaps Ivo and Osprey weren't wrong about the bees. Just seeing them once had an effect on these two.

I swayed. I could feel the vision coming this time. I hadn't seen one in so long that I almost longed for it. If only I'd thought to send a bee with Retger or Zayana. I still could – but I didn't even know where to send it. I could send them through the whole city. But then I'd blackout even more and it was already happening too often.

Darkness crashed over me at the same moment that I heard Oman curse. I could feel my body being dragged as I slipped into my vision.

I was seeing from a perspective that didn't feel like my bee.

I was on the docks as the boats landed. Dozens of them. Filled with Claws armed to the teeth. I stormed down the dock as they fanned out around me. Out of the corner of my eye, I noticed a huge shining metal brazier and in its brass side I saw Juste Montpetit, striking a brazen pose, his shirt completely unbuttoned so that I could see his gleaming chest and the hexagons of my honeycomb in his belly. His snake looped around his neck and rolled down his outstretched hand as he pointed toward the city.

"Raze it to the ground. We'll have no rebellions on the soil of the Winged Empire." His words were ice and fire and they seared through me.

Raze the city? He was mad. I could barely catch my breath as his Wings and Claws surged forward, blades spinning in front of them like they thought they were on parade, but beauty did not dull the edge of their measured attack. As soon as they left the docks, their spinning blades hit flesh, and sprays of red splashed across snowy embroidery, staining blue coats purple and dark. In the middle of it, the eye of a storm, the calm before murder, Juste strode past the brazier, his face as still and beautiful as it was on the coin. He was the opposite of Osprey in every way – cruel and cold where Osprey ran hot and passionate. Ambitious and self-serving where Osprey would stab knives into himself to spare me. They faced different directions in this world.

My vision snapped back to my body. Oman towed me along behind him, grunting at the weight.

"I can stand," I gasped, clawing my way to my feet. When did my hands get so dirty?

"We're there," he said, tiredly. "The Oriole Fountain."

I looked up, gasping in relief. We'd made it this far. Beside me, Dahn sagged as we took a moment to try to drink from the fountain.

"The monastery should be near," I managed but I was distracted. Was that what the coin had meant? That Osprey and Juste faced opposite directions even though it seemed like they were on the same side? The image of Juste's cold face flooded my mind – his big blue eyes as pitiless as the sea. But then my eyes narrowed as another face filled my mind – another set of hard blue eyes, but these ones were ravaged by pain and guilt.

I froze.

Beside me, the boys were gasping, catching their breath, bathing their faces in cool fountain water, but I was stunned into rigid silence. How could I have failed to see it?

He'd given me the coin so desperately – as if it was a message. And that was because it was a message. It was the story of the two brothers. Twin brothers and one of them would rule. I'd been distracted by the different color of their skin. But they were the same age, weren't they? And they had the same blue eyes. One gave the orders. One received them. But Juste had never treated Osprey like a normal Wing in the time I'd seen them together. He'd never just ignored him or ordered him around – it had always been with purpose.

What if the Emperor had two sons born to him the same year? What if one was legitimate and one was not? Tradition said he'd kill the other heir or let his son do it. But maybe he was waiting to see what might happen. And then one of them had Hatched. And he'd been immediately tied up with the souls of children and told that any deviation from his orders would bring their deaths.

Of course. No one would do that to just a normal boy. But they'd do it to a potential heir to the throne, wouldn't they? To keep him in line. Because he was the spare. And when Juste was crowned, he would be killed like every other sibling to an emperor had been.

An icy chill tore through me.

And I would be there to see it all because the crown prince was intent on making me his bride. And Ivo thought he'd done that just to torment Osprey further.

The blood drained from my face. Suddenly, everything made sense to me. But knowing wasn't enough. I needed to act. There had to be some way to pry the rest of that feather from Osprey's chest. There had to be some way to free him from this.

"There it is," Dahn said, wincing as he tried to point at something. I shook myself and followed his gesture to see a low stone spire. "The monastery."

We stumbled toward it, all three exhausted and battered. I limped, my left leg damaged by a stone shot by a sling hours ago. It had hit the side of my knee and every step sent a shot of pain above and below the injury. No time to stop and check it. We could only move forward.

Wind roared around us, and I glanced behind me to see a ball of flame shoot up from the dye merchant's shop.

Forbidding take it!

The wind was already fanning the flames, and it was blowing in our direction. This was my worst fear – that the records would be burned before I could even access them.

We stumbled to the stone building. It was smaller than I would have thought, a slender tower that ended abruptly in a jagged line of stone.

It did not look like the rest of the city. It looked almost as if it had been birthed of the rock, rather than built here. Someone had carefully carved stone totems of birds and placed them around the low moss-covered entrance, but it seemed to me as if they weren't placed for decoration, but in a ring to ward something off. What was in the building that was so dangerous it had to be kept inside?

I squinted harder, seeing a twisted form behind all the birds. Could that have been the body of a snake, the head knocked off and replaced by that carved eagle? And on the other side, another snake, hidden by a swan? I didn't have time for chills, and yet one ran up my spine all the same.

"How do we get inside?" I asked, looking for a door.

There didn't seem to be one. The monastery was placed at the very center of a small hedge-shrouded garden. Each of its eight sides were covered in thick lichen – so thick that it obscured something that was carved in the stone – and they were identical, except for where the totems had been placed. No one side looked more like it should have a door than any other. I thought I saw scuff marks leading up to one of the carved panels on one side, but it could easily have been my imagination.

"I've never heard of anyone going inside," Oman said with a shrug. "It's just here."

"Someone cuts the hedges," I argued.

The boys just shrugged.

"And it's called a monastery. So that suggests there are monks."

They shrugged again. Very helpful.

It was getting hotter as the fire licked toward us and then a cry echoed down the street. I glanced over my shoulder and froze. A Claw stood in the center of the street, pointing at us. He called behind him just as dozens more emerged from around the corner. Fire, pursuit, and no way in.

I ground my teeth together.

"You got me here," I said to Oman and Dahn. "Now run. This is my battle to fight."

They exchanged a glance.

"You can tell people what you saw – that there are bees in Far Stones."

They nodded their heads to that, and Oman made something like a salute in response.

"We'll tell everyone."

I clapped them on the shoulders, glad I'd finally found some way to convince them to go. This wasn't their fight.

"Be safe," I said.

"We'll tell everyone," Dahn said, his eyes as fiery as the flush in his cheeks. "Everyone."

Just as long as he did it a long way from here.

"Go."

I gave him a gentle shove and breathed a sigh of relief when he finally turned and stumbled down the street, away from both the Claws and the flames. At least I wouldn't get them killed with me. At least I could say that much.

I was glad that Zayana and Retger hadn't come here with me. I wouldn't have to watch them die, either. I placed my hand against one wall of the monastery and concentrated my thoughts. The strangest sensation – like a snake slithering across my palm – filled my mind. I jerked my hand back and it was gone. But now, through the lichen, I could see words glowing and I froze, swallowing down bile.

We keep what we catch.

Stories and souls.

Dreams and Sight.

Come in and Fetch.

Hearts and tales.

Hopes so bright.

Open with Blood,

Pay our price.

Bind your eyes.

Lose what you Loved,

Empty and cold.

It all grows old.

Lay bare your Desire,

Great or small,

Gain it twice.

Burn on our Pyre

Bright and hot,

Soul made naught.

Ominous and spooky. I was already regretting coming here and this only made it worse, but at least one thing was pretty clear about that door. It opened in a different kind of way. "Open with blood," it said. I decided to take it at face value. I took my sword, cut my palm, and placed it against the poem. There was a grinding sound of stone on stone but nothing else.

I'd put my blood here, wasn't that enough?

There was another cry from the Claws behind me – louder this time.

They were almost here. I needed to think. Think. Aella! Think!

A door that didn't open. A monastery with no books. A useless dead end. I closed my eyes and leaned my forehead against the panel, trying to think.

And fell through the wall.

CHAPTER SEVENTEEN

I gasped, stumbling, shocked by my sudden fall, but I managed to keep my feet, knife still in my hand. I'd expected a tomb after the way this place looked from the outside.

Instead, I found a library. A very full library. Books filled the available space, shelves climbing upward as far as the eye could see, supported by carved bird totems and accessible by towering ladders and tiny railed platforms. Even the shelves were a tribute to the Winged Empire with little songbirds clutching vines carved into the shelf faces. Below, the books were set in leaning stacks or sprawled out over bookstands in all their open, tumbled glory. I could spend many weeks here. But I didn't have that long.

The library was full of more than just books and tension rang through the small building like a clattering bell. Five men and women dressed in long, gauzy white robes stood before me, their hair pulled back and corded into braids. They were arranged in a half-circle, their faces showing looks ranging from indifference to pure judgment.

And I wasn't the only visitor there.

"Retger!" I gasped.

"Shrikeling, you made it." Relief filled his features as he turned to quickly hug me. "When we lost you in the chaos, we both feared the worst. I went back for you, but you'd been swept away. I know I said to meet at the inn, but I had a premonition that you'd keep on going."

Zayana looked relieved, too, her bird's flames grew a little brighter from where he hovered just over her shoulder. I saw the nearest monk flinch at the sight.

"How did you get here?" I asked. "And when did you get here?"

"We fought our way through," Retger said, but there was frustration on his face. "We arrived almost an hour ago, but these monks will not help us. And I'm getting nervous. It's getting louder outside."

"The fires are close," I breathed and he nodded tightly, seeming to read my mood and determination just from those few words.

"As we've been saying," one of the monks said. "This monastery is not open to the public. Though we feel for your plight in the chaos of the city, we cannot allow you to disturb this place. It has been here since before the founding of the Empire's colony on Far Stones and here it will remain long past any temporary turmoil. No weapons or magic or breathed threats will change our minds."

"We aren't here to flee the violence," Retger protested impatiently and it sounded like he was repeating himself. Had he really threatened them?

I laid a hand on his arm, my brows furrowing as I stepped forward. "Since before the arrival of the Winged Empire here? So my eyes did not deceive me. You placed totems around this place to ward off whatever is inside. And this very tower grew out of the land. I can see how it twists up like the Forbidding itself."

Fear lit the eyes of the monk who had been speaking and

around her, the four others made the sign of the bird.

"Peace," she said, to me. "Peace. Do not speak of what you don't know."

I took a step forward, sheathing my knife but crossing my arms over my chest. "If I don't know about this, then you need to tell me. We came here looking for insight into the times of the early settlement here. This seems like the exact place to get that information."

The monk seemed to relax. There was a smugness to her smile when she said, "Our written records only reach back to the time after the city of Glorious Ingvar was built."

I smiled but not in a friendly way. "Your written records. That's the key, isn't it? You said this place was here before you even arrived. So, let's talk about unwritten records."

Her face paled. Her companions were shaking their heads unconsciously, bodies stiff.

"Are there unwritten records of a time before the Empire of War and Wings took this monastery? Perhaps they speak of a general. One with two ravens."

The monk paled even further until I thought she might pass out. I watched her throat bob as she swallowed before steeling her face.

"Why would there be records of that here?"

Behind me, Retger snorted. "Why indeed. But if there weren't records, I doubt you'd look so pale!"

I was out of patience. There was a muffled crash from outside. We didn't have time to pick at their words.

"This monastery is about to burn with all your precious books inside. Our time here is limited, and I need answers," I said grimly. "Lead me to your records of this time before. Or I will show you the same grit I showed the Claws outside."

"Our monastery cannot be burned," the monk said smugly. "We are not of the outside world."

But the others looked less certain.

My bees were out before I'd even made the conscious decision to release them. They swirled out from my hands and centered around the monk as I took an aggressive step forward.

"Neither am I, monk. Show me these records."

She exchanged a look with the other monks and one of them made the sign of the bird a second time.

"Bees," the other monk said. "As prophesied."

The others looked frightened, their eyes flicking from me to Retger and then their leader. She shook her head as if she pitied me.

"If you want access to our hidden records, then access them all you like. It is not we who will pay the price for that," she said mildly.

I drew my bees back to me, nodding. "Good. Can you point me in the direction of the records concerning this general?"

She snorted. "He was the same kind of fool you are and faced the same kind of fate. But don't worry. The unwritten records record his ending as surely as they will record yours."

I glanced at Retger. "Why do I feel like she's going to brick me up in a hole under this library?"

"Because she's being intentionally creepy," Retger said, drawing his sword. "It's not a survival trait."

"Peace!" The monk's hands were up, all smugness fading away. "Peace. We – we monks, that is – will not hurt you. It's your very request that carries the risk and if you choose to go into the heart of the tower and see what is hidden here, then it is the tower you must fear and not us. Yes, we have a library here, but this monastery was created for two reasons – to contain the power within and to obscure it from prying eyes. This place is not safe for mortals. It houses a tendril of that great entity you call the Forbidding and through that tendril, you may access the hidden tower and the mind behind the evil of this world. We live – every single day – in service of the good work of keeping people from that fate. Your ignorance – while horribly fascinating – is dangerous to you and to our cause. So, no, we do not mean you any harm and that is precisely why we have tried to warn you away."

There was a roar outside and the sound of something crashing. I felt my body tense. We were running out of time. Totems wouldn't keep Claws out and they wouldn't keep flames out.

"Let's just get this done," Retger muttered from beside me, watching the ceiling nervously. Zayana made the sign of the bird, her eyes turned up with his. "Before this place comes crashing down in us."

"What do you mean by 'hidden' tower? The broken tower is clear to see from outside," I pressed. I was in a hurry, but that didn't mean I could just rush in. I needed to learn to think things through first.

The monks shuffled uneasily. "The tower you see is just the physical shell around the real tower. The real tower is invisible – a thing of spirit and cloud. Anything trapped within – or that which emanates from what is trapped within – is also invisible."

"Wait …" Retger said. "Trapped?"

The monks seemed to stand taller. "We are trying to warn you. It is possible to be trapped within the tower. And if you enter it, we expect you will be trapped, too. The Forbidding is not to be tangled with. It is to be contained and defended against. Even we – who know the secrets of the Forbidding Tower – even we do not enter it."

"But it's inside that tower that we'll find the records of what came before, correct?" I said, steeling myself. I was going to have to do this. "It's there that we'll find what happened to the general?"

The monks exchanged a look before the lead monk sighed again.

"Yes," she said.

"Then I'm going in." I turned to Retger and Zayana. "Can you guard my back? I really don't want to be bricked into a basement somewhere.

Retger snorted. "You won't be. On my blood and the honor of House Shrike, sister, I will guard your back. I will be there for you."

I nodded, satisfied. "I'm ready."

"No one is ever ready," the monk countered. "But we will grant you the right to die on your own terms. Come."

I stepped forward and Retger stepped behind me.

"Only the girl. If you wish to defend her, warrior of House Shrike, then you and your Wing will do it from here."

I noticed Zayana's blush and shy look toward Retger at being labeled his. That was fast. Though I could hardly judge her for it. After all, I had fallen almost that quickly for … wait, that was undecided, Aella! I was not going to admit that – even to myself. Not right now when I needed a clear mind.

I cleared my throat, dislodging the thought.

"Lead on, monk."

She led me between the shelves. They curled like the shell of a snail, spiraling into the center where a pillar stood – carved of black stone. It was a roiling pillar of interwoven snakes, swirling up from the floor into the sky and broken just above my head. On the pillar, the same words were written as on the door of the monastery.

She read the words aloud in a hallowed tone.

"We keep what we catch.

Stories and souls.

Dreams and Sight.

Come in and Fetch.

Hearts and tales.

Hopes so bright.

Open with Blood,

Pay our price.

Bind your eyes.

Lose what you Loved,

Empty and cold.

It all grows old.

Lay bare your Desire,

Great or small,

Gain it twice.

Burn on our Pyre

Bright and hot,

Soul made naught."

"More blood?" I inquired.

"If only that was all it demanded," the monk said dryly. "No, not this time. This time, think of the thing you are here to retrieve. But know that wanting a thing does not mean you'll get a thing. And if you fail to be true – if what you want is not what you think you want – then your desire may warp what you are ultimately given."

"That sounds dangerous." My palms were already sweating.

"Of course, it is. None of us truly knows our hearts."

"And what makes the Forbidding so generous as to grant desires?"

Her laugh was harsh. "Generous? It will take far more from you than it gives, and I doubt it will give you what you want. It never has in the past."

The monastery shook as a battering sound filled the room.

"I'd tell you that time is short," the monk said, "but I think you already know that."

Chapter Eighteen

How could you make your motives pure?

I tried to concentrate on wanting to free the general – but it was hard not to let that get tangled up with wanting to defeat the Winged Empire and as soon as that struck my mind, it was hard not to think about Osprey or how I could be free of him hunting me – which would mean setting him to be free. What would he do if he was free? Would I ever see him again?

I took a deep breath – tried not to think of those things – and concentrated solely on the general. Victore. I needed him free.

Skies have mercy. Stars have mercy. It was like before when I sensed that there was some great presence listening to me. I reached upward with my heart calling for help. Grant me the clarity of heart to enter this door.

I took a deep breath, concentrating all my thought on Victore and stepped forward, placing my forehead against the pillar and closing my eyes yet again.

I stumbled into what I could only guess was the invisible tower. The floor was glass – or at least, it was translucent – and it glowed a rich golden orange as if there was a fire deep below that I could not see. The walls appeared to be woven of living black vines, which twisted and moved as I watched them, forming stairs that twisted up around the walls in a spiral and sprouting red flowers at the end of their twisting tendrils, only to let them die – living a full lifetime in the blink of an eye – and then re-sprouting them again.

My heart sped up. I hoped that time was not twisted here, that it wasn't going as fast as those flowers. What if this place was like the stories where someone entered a magic cave and came back an old man later that afternoon?

BUT WHAT ISSS TIME?

A voice spoke in my mind. It hissed, stretching its "S's" out too far. It felt almost as if a snake had crept up my spine and burrowed into the base of my skull and was lying within, whispering to me.

WE KEEP WHAT WE CATCH LITTLE BEE AND WE CAUGHT YOU.

Caught? I couldn't afford to be caught right now. I had people depending on me. I turned around the tower base, but there was nothing here but glowing light and a twisting, moving, staircase of vines that climbed so high up the tower wall that it twisted into darkness.

I was trapped.

WE TAKE WHAT YOU LOVE, BUZZING BEE. AND YOU LOVE TO BE FREE.

Everyone loved being free.

YOU LOVE IT MORE.

I shivered and then turned that into a spasm of shaking as I tried to dislodge the feeling of the voice in my mind – but it would not go. Was it really possible that it was somehow the spirit of the Forbidding?

SSSEE WHAT WE MEAN? WE ARE TANGLED IN YOU – ROOTED IN YOUR HEART WHERE THERE IS ALREADY A TANGLE OF USSS SEEDED.

I felt like I might be ill. My head was spinning.

A tangle of what?

WHAT YOU CALL THE FORBIDDING. IT IS IN YOUR HEART. IT LURKSSS WHERE IT CAN NOT BE DESTROYED. BECAUSSSE TO DESTROY USSS ISSS TO DESTROY YOU.

A wave of nausea washed over me. I had better not have some of that in me. I couldn't stomach the thought. It was all I could do to pull myself together enough to talk to my own spirit. Remember, Aella, just because a creepy voice says something, doesn't mean it's true.

YOU ARE ALREADY OUR SSSLAVESS. ALL THAT REMAINSS ISS TO DECIDE HOW TO MAKE YOU DANCCCE.

"I was told you'd give me my desire," I said boldly. Enough of this nonsense. Enough of this talk.

IT'S DESSIRESS YOU WANT? THEN CLIMB THE SSTAIRSSS.

I swallowed, looking at the moving stairs. There was no rail, they merely followed the curve of the tower wall, made entirely of tangle strands. It would be like walking up a staircase of Forbidding. You'd have to be crazy to do it.

CRAZY OR NOTHING. CLIMB OR ROT.

I looked around the base of the tower.

THERE IS NO WAY OUT EXCEPT UP.

I'd come this far. I could do the rest, right?

Skies, bear me upward to your embrace. Let me know your depths and eddies. Fill me with the courage of the west wind and the light spirit of the laughing zephyr.

I reached into my re-ordered self – the me who had been folded and kneaded the last time I encountered old magic. There was a resonance in me as if I recognized all of this. It calmed me, somehow, making me feel as though I could manage what came next. It didn't show me any visions, though. Maybe in this place, that wasn't possible.

My whole body was shaking as I took the first step, despite my new courage. My foot settled onto something solid and I breathed a sigh of relief.

Too soon. The tangled step moved to cup my foot, adjusting itself just a little higher. My stomach dropped and I reached for the wall to steady myself. The vines making the wall reached back, tangling around my hand. I cried out and pulled my hand back losing my balance and nearly falling off the step.

CLIMB.

Great. Just great. I either had to accept that the Forbidding was going to interact with me as I climbed, or I had to leave emptyhanded.

THERE ISSS NO LEAVING. YET.

And those stairs were not safe.

SSSAFETY. THE EVER PRESSSENT ENEMY OF ADVENTURE. ONE CANNOT BE FREE AND ALSO SSAFE. WHICH DO YOU PREFER, HONEY BEE?

That was easy. I thought of Juste holding me captive, threatening me with forced marriage and the removal of my tongue. The snake in my mind seemed to like the memory, hissing with pleasure as I replayed it in my mind.

"Freedom," I said aloud. "I'd rather make my own bad choices and suffer for them than suffer for choices thrust on to me."

Skies preserve me. I was reaching now with every ounce of hope that I had.

A BEE BUZZING AGAINST THE GLASS. A FUTILE WISSSSH.

"It's not futile. We're made of our choices. There has to be freedom to be human at all."

THEN CLIMB.

I took another step, gritting my teeth with determination as I climbed. One more. I flung my arms out to the side, swaying as I tried to keep my balance on steps that swayed with me.

Skies have mercy. Stars have mercy.

As I climbed, I felt the snake in my mind … sifting … rummaging somehow in my mind as it hissed. I did not like this. I wasn't sure I believed it was some kind of extension of the Forbidding, but I definitely didn't like it.

YOU DON'T THINK WE ARE YOUR PRECIOUS ENEMY? YOU THINK WE ARE LIMITED TO MINDLESS CLAWING ALONG THE GROUND? AND YET YOU HAVE TAKEN OUR PATHS UNDER THE GROUND.

I shivered. I thought those paths were from the snake people, not the Forbidding.

STOLEN FROM US. BUT WE REACH FARTHER THAN YOU CAN GUESS. WE REFORM THE EARTH. WE TAKE BACK WHAT IS OURS.

Pain shot through my mind and I stumbled, catching myself against the tangled wall. Little tendrils shot out, stabilizing me and for the first time, I didn't recoil in horror. I was too busy trying to keep my head as images burst across my mind. It was like when the snake people put me in their temple – but worse.

THAT IS A TINY TENDRIL OF US, TOO. BUT WE ARE STRONGER HERE. THE PEOPLE OF THIS PLACE HAVE ACCOMMODATED TO US. THEY ADAPT AND LEARN. WE LIKE THAT.

I barely heard the voice, I was so caught up in the visions crashing over me. I saw images of people fighting off the tangle of the Forbidding. People dressed in clothing I couldn't identify. People with complexions and hair I'd never seen before. Weapons I'd never seen before. Perhaps they were places that the Winged Empire had never found, filled with strange people fighting our same battle against the Forbidding. It was almost comforting to think of others fighting the same battle.

Until I saw a bright bird flying over the tangle of Forbidding as it crawled across the sea. A pair of Imperial Tern ships raced across the waves as a huge bluish-white raven plunged toward the mass of Forbidding, talons outstretched, a scream ripping from its throat. It ripped at the snatching tangles, keeping the Forbidding from catching the stern of the slower ship. On the deck, a man in a short Wing coat braced himself on the rail, teeth clenched, and hands splayed outward.

Had the Forbidding crossed the sea? Was it attacking ships as they sailed? My heart clenched in my chest and in my mind the tendril of Forbidding hissed happily.

I took another step upward and I was rocked in place as a new image scored a path through my mind – the image of hundreds of Claws, fighting and slashing along a line of turf as a roiling mass of Forbidding crept across the land. The Claws were giving ground, their blue and white uniforms muddy and torn, eyes wild.

My heart seized in my throat. That was not Far Stones. It was not our rocky land. It was a place rich and verdant, thick with plants whose leaves were larger than I was. The mainland. The continent.

And if the Forbidding was attacking there. And attacking in the sea. And attacking peoples I'd never even heard stories of before. Then what could stop it?

NOTHING.

That – perhaps – was true.

"And where do you come from, creeping Forbidding?" I whispered as I mounted another step. "And where are you going."

THE HEARTS OF MAN.

"And what will you do when all hearts are yours?"

BREATHE.

Well, that wasn't creepy at all. Not at all.

"What are you?"

DON'T YOU KNOW YET?

I didn't know. But I had an idea. I had a vague, unformed idea in my mind of ancient magic, not tuned to birds or bees or snakes in particular, but reaching out and capturing people, bending and folding them to see what they were made of and planting little seeds in them. A magic with a curious mind.

A thought washed over me and I clamped it down hard. I didn't dare let myself dwell on anything that might defeat the Forbidding – not here where it could read my mind.

YOU CAN'T HIDE FROM ME. ALL RACESS PASS AWAY AND ARE REBORN NEW AND THEN THOSE PASSS TOO. BUT THE SSSNAKE ISSS ENDLESSS.

That was a lot of hissing for me. I stumbled up another stair. The shadows were closing in now, thicker and deeper. But I was playing by the rules and I could only hope that the Forbidding was playing by them, too.

YOU WILL GET YOUR DESIRE. WILL IT BE WHAT YOU THINK IT IS?

The general. I was here for the general.

IS THAT WHERE YOUR HEART IS? TRULY?

"Where is your heart?" I asked, flipping it around, refusing to let that terrible entity sift any further through my mind.

DEEP IN THE DARK, DOWN IN THE STONE,

FOLLOW THE EARTHBEAT AND FIND MY HOME.

It seemed to love poetry. Which was a strange quirk for a mindless force.

WE ARE NEITHER MINDLESS NOR A FORCE. KNOW US AND LIVE.

I shuddered at the same moment that my head smacked into something above me. I reached up and pushed against something solid, but the tendrils of Forbidding pushed, too, and the trapdoor swung upward.

I couldn't stop the burst of hope that filled me.

I slid the bolt back and opened the trap door.

But I lost my mental focus as I lifted it and accidentally thought of Osprey. Of how I needed to get him untethered from Juste before I could fight the Forbidding properly.

Laughter echoed in my mind.

HE'S TIED UP BY HIS OWN SEED OF FORBIDDING IN HIS HEART. JUST AS ALL HUMANS ARE. THERE IS NO UNTANGLING WHAT HAS BEEN TIED.

But that wasn't true, was it? I'd untangled things before.

I pulled myself the last step up to through the trap door to the top of the tower and in my mind, I was seeing fire – all the fires I'd set at the heart of trees and beasts – the fires that stopped the Forbidding. There were ways to stop it – if only I dared.

CHAPTER NINETEEN

I stumbled up into the light and gasped. I was face-to-face with a man who had once been powerful and very tall. Now, he was stooped and gaunt. He gaped at me, his beard – long and bedraggled – blew in the breeze. The trapdoor opened onto a slick floor and a cage. Both floor and cage were made of something tangled and as the tangle turned from floor into walls, it became translucent. There were gaps in the weaving, but none of them were big enough for me to pass, never mind the man.

I staggered when I took in the view around the tower. I could see the whole city. Every bit of it. We were so high above the broken top of the visible tower that my knees shook. Every single person in the city should have been able to see this tower. And yet it was utterly hidden from view.

"The blue coats take back the city. They broke the rebels with a Veturian Maneuver. I've tried that one myself," the man said through chapped lips, his voice rusty and squeaking. He coughed and when he spoke again it was clear. "It was a valiant effort by the people here. Valiant. I've watched them fall all day. One by one. They were close to turning the tide before the ships landed. But Veturian always works on a rebellion."

He gestured and I gasped at the sight of Juste's ships in the harbor. There were more of them than I thought could have arrived from Karkatua. He couldn't have received reinforcements already, could he?

Victore was watching them, more intent on what went on below than on me – his would-be savior.

"Are you Victore?" I asked cautiously.

"Victore of House Raven," he said, his words heavy with emotions and memories that layered to make them opaque.

There was a flurry of wings above us and then two ravens darted between the bars and landed – one on his right shoulder and the other on the top of his balding head. "Too narrow for me to leap and end my torment, but not too narrow for Sorrow and Trouble."

He reached up and stroked the birds affectionately. One of the two dropped something in his palm. I realized – in horror – that it was a small mouse. He popped it into his mouth and I barely swallowed down my bile as he chewed it, crunching the bones, and swallowing the entire mouse before speaking again.

"They can bring some for you, too. Sorrow is an excellent hunter. And I will be glad for the company, prisoners though we are."

My stomach was still turning. I fought down nausea. "They feed you?"

"And they bring me drink, too, don't you, Trouble?" He patted the head of the raven on his head.

It took me a moment to shake myself back to why I was here.

"I'm here to free you. We need to go – before the tower catches fire."

He walked to the edge and peered down. "The smoke will be a problem. Hard to breathe. Hard for the ravens to find food."

"We need to go," I repeated. Should I catch his hand in mine and compel him? I was worried that he would react poorly to that. He was keeping his distance.

"It won't burn. This tower isn't of the world. Is but isn't. Real but unreal. Alive but dead."

"Even if it doesn't burn, our window is closing."

"Many years I have survived here on this nest above the world with only my manifestations to share my cell, isn't that right Sorrow and Trouble," he mused, looking affectionately at his manifestations.

"And now those years are over."

"There is no way out." His voice sounded hollow. "And no way to leap to your death. Put a little piece of your mind away somewhere safe and let the rest go mad."

Was he mad?

He began to hum to himself.

This was the worst prison rescue ever. Frustrated, I turned to the trapdoor to show him the way out and realized it was closed and hidden now – under the tangle of Forbidding that made the floor of this tower. I hurried over to it and when I reached for the trapdoor the tangles of Forbidding reached up and grasped my hand.

IS THIS YOUR DESIRE? DESIRES COME AT A COST.

The voice was still there. I should not feel comforted by that, but I was.

"Come on, Victore. We need to flee while we can."

"There's nowhere to flee to. It crept up over the hills,

swallowing us up one by one. There was nowhere to flee to. It was already in our hearts."

That was far too close to what the Forbidding had told me – if the mind in this tower really was the Forbidding.

"I fought long and hard. Led my people. But the Forbidding takes no prisoners. Once it was benign – or perhaps even good – there are still places where it folds that goodness into you. Oh, I've felt that. I felt it. But this tower is not one of those places. This tower has felt the creeping corruption turn it to evil. It was evil when I was placed here and has only grown more so. No longer do I lead men. These days, I'm lucky to lead my own thoughts."

"That's why I'm here," I said firmly. "The men need you to lead them again."

His head whipped around to me, eyes bright and haunted. "It was in the night as I slept that someone slipped in. Put a sack over my head. Bound my mouth and hands. Dragged me from my rooms."

"Please," I pled. "You can tell all of it to me as we flee. But we need to go now!"

"I never saw faces. Never saw hands. Never saw anything. Never heard anything. And when I finally tore off my bonds, I was here. Who betrayed me, little bird?" His eyes were hard on mine. "Who ripped me from the earth and left me in this nest?"

"We can find out. We can find out all of it – but not if we stay here." I was surprised to realize tears were pricking my eyes.

"There, there, little girl."

He took a step toward me and a stab of fear shot down my spine. I wanted him to follow me, but he followed like someone about to spring.

I reached for the trapdoor and the floor reached for me.

A sound of terror broke through his lips, his eyes wide as he watched the Forbidding greet me.

"It's better than staying here forever, don't you think?" I coaxed, but I wasn't looking at him, I was looking at the tentacles moving from the trapdoor handle to my hand. They tangled around my wrist and then with a snick the trapdoor opened, and the golden darkness below yawned wide.

I reached back and firmly took Victore's hand. He tried to snatch it away but after a heartbeat, it went limp and his head bowed down.

"You take me to my death. You come at last to do their bidding and trap my soul."

"I'm rescuing you," I reminded him, but he only shook his head.

He needed something more, I could see it in the hunch of his shoulders.

"Come to me, bees," I whispered.

I opened my palm and held it under his face so his bowed head could see as I breathed out and let out one of my bees. Just one. He danced across my palm manically.

Victore's head snapped up and his brown eyes looked into mine – piercing and filled with a tangle of emotions I couldn't place.

"A bee. She holds a bee."

"Come with me," I urged, taking a step down into the

embrace of the Forbidding. I felt hot all over but I couldn't concentrate on that.

He followed me, his eyes locked onto my bee.

Could he still lead an army like this? He seemed to know what was happening below him, but he leapt from shadows. And he ate mice whole. I clenched my jaw, trying to avoid remembering that. I didn't want to vomit. Whether he could or not, I was committed to this now, and leaving him here to continue existing like this was unthinkable. I ignored the burning feeling in my hands and head and drew him onward.

I led him down the moving, reaching stairs, holding his hand even as he quivered and shuddered behind me. He must think I was leading him into the depths of hell, but still, he followed, his eyes never wavering from my bee. His ravens came with us, still perched on his head and shoulder like grim guardians of his hollow mind.

We reached the bottom step and the voice of the Forbidding ripped through me.

LAY BARE YOUR DESIRE,

GREAT OR SMALL,

GAIN IT TWICE.

BURN ON OUR PYRE

BRIGHT AND HOT,

SOUL MADE NAUGHT.

I'd already laid bare my desire – to save the general. Heat flared in me – so hot and bright now that I could barely breathe.

WHAT'S REALLY YOUR DESIRE?

I froze, my foot on the last step. Of course, freeing the general was my desire. I'd been very clear. Was the Forbidding changing its mind now?

WE PLAY BY THE RULES OF THE TOWER. WE TOOK SOMETHING FROM YOU. WE GIVE SOMETHING BACK.

What had they taken from me? My heart began to race.

WAIT AND YOU WILL SEE.

There was a glee to those words. My left wrist burned hot as the sun.

WE GIVE BACK YOUR DESIRES – TANGLED THOUGH THEY ARE.

I stumbled down the last step, feeling agony burst through my chest, so much pain that I couldn't think, couldn't talk, could only grasp Victore's hand as the floor rose up in hundreds of vine-like tentacles and pushed me toward the wall of the tower. Pain. So much pain.

What had I said I wanted? I'd asked for Victore, hadn't I? I reached for the sky and stars.

The floor shoved and I was pushed right through the wall, gasping, and half-sobbing as the pain began to fade. I clutched at my chest with one hand and at Victore with the other as the realization rippled through me. I might have asked for Victore but I'd never once stopped thinking of how desperate I was to get Osprey free. That desperate hope filled me even now. I didn't think I could let it go even if I wanted to.

Someone gasped and I moaned, forcing myself from where I'd stumbled to my feet. My wrist hurt. My chest hurt. I felt bound up by unfulfilled desire and desperate hope and in that strange state I looked up straight into the blue eyes of Osprey.

CHAPTER TWENTY

WHAT'S REALLY YOUR DESIRE?

The words echoed in my mind as I felt the blood rush out of my face just from looking at him.

His lips parted and the toothpick dropped from them. I reached out and caught it from the air. I didn't dare let him get the first words – or actions! – in. Not now that I knew.

I knew he was trapped by something inside himself and that he could be freed. But he wouldn't be freed by a dagger digging out the feather. I'd need something better than that to free him. There was so much that stood between us, it was like an impenetrable wall – that he was brother to the crown prince, that the Forbidding was everywhere on every shore and deep inside him, that there was some kind of pull between us that made it impossible for us not to look deeply into each other's eyes as if running a tally of what had happened to the other since we last saw each other. And this time I wasn't going to run while he chased me. This time, I was going to do the chasing.

"If you must take me to your brother, then you may," I said calmly.

He pressed his lips together, his brow furrowing at my words.

Behind him, I saw that Ivo was leaning against the bookshelf, sweat pouring from his forehead, his blade wobbling in a circle as he guarded Osprey's back from my brother. Retger crouched, back against the other bookshelf, breathing hard. He had a fresh bruise on his cheek and Zayana was tucked in behind him, safe from danger. She kept looking from him to Ivo like she couldn't understand what had happened or what she should do.

Books lay scattered everywhere and more than one shelf was toppled. Around the perimeter of the room, the monks stood still as statues, hands up in a warding gesture or covering horrified mouths. Retger's arm was bleeding and Ivo was hunched over a wound. There had been a fight.

I looked over Osprey. He stood tall and straight, but heat curled up from him like mist and his blade was streaked in blood.

"You came for me? Then take me," I said grimly. "But leave the others here – all of them. That fulfills your orders, doesn't it?"

His mouth snapped shut and his throat bobbed as he swallowed down whatever he was going to say. He swallowed the words, but he couldn't swallow the look in his eyes that seemed to be eating me up.

"He tried to hurt Zayana. You can't go with him," Retger said through clenched teeth. "That's our enemy no matter what love-lorn looks he gives you."

I held up a hand, impatient. "If he wanted to hurt you, Os would have torn you to pieces already. He is clearly holding himself back."

I drew Victore around me and gently guided him to Retger. The others still had their weapons up and ready for battle, but I was determined not to let that worry me despite a wobble in my knees.

"We need Victore. The Single Wing needs their general." I

met Retger's eyes. "Take him to the place where my bee found you." Victore would be safe with my family but I didn't want to mention them aloud. "I will join you as soon as I can."

"I won't leave you with these madmen." My brother's voice was raw.

"Madman," I corrected. "You're taking Wing Ivo with you."

"But he's our enemy, Aella. What kind of brother would I be if I agreed to that? The Wing will stay here and you will come with me where I can keep you safe."

"I'm no enemy of yours, boy," Ivo said, his chest still heaving like he'd just been running or fighting hard. "But when you come at me all slash-dash-crash like a carabao in a potter's shed, then I'll put up my blade and do what I have to. I love liberty and freedom and truth and justice. And if that's what you love, then we're blood brothers. Stop slashing at me and I'll stop slashing at you. Plain and simple."

Retger watched him with the same careful uncertainty that I always felt – like he couldn't tell if he was serious or crazy.

"And he's Zayana's Guide," I said gently. "He won't hurt her. He'll only help her."

Retger nodded uncertainly. "He can come if you want him, but you're coming, too."

"You know the way to get there quickly," I said, raising my eyebrows to try to remind him of the undertrails. "I'll find you on that path."

Nothing about escaping. Nothing about joining them if I could. I didn't dare tip my hand. I had to be quick and I had to be smart. I'd had enough of being driven by the winds around me. It was time for me to steer this ship.

He shook his head again and I made a chopping motion with my hand.

"You must let me do this, brother. It's something only I can do and if you don't get the general to safety, then what will happen to the revolution? We must be relentless."

"It feels wrong to leave you, Shrikeling," Retger said, but Zayana reached out and caught his hand and he relaxed just a hair. "You should go with the Wing and Zay and the general and I'll stay here and deal with whatever this Wing wants from you."

"I agree," Ivo rumbled. "No need to surrender just because things have become difficult."

I shook my head. "I'm not surrendering. I'm fighting in my own way."

"Aella." My name on Retger's lips was a plea.

I glanced at Osprey who had remained perfectly still this whole time, his bright eyes never leaving me, his body trembling as if he was holding back from saying something. He kept looking me up and down as if he was trying to assess me.

"It's a task only I can take on, Retger," I said, keeping my voice low and trying to sound certain. I could see he was crumbling in the face of my certainty. Even now, it might end in disaster, but one way or another, this endless chase had to stop. It would have been better if I'd had time to lay a trap, but our trap last time hadn't worked. I'd just have to do what I could. "And they need you. You have to go."

He made a frustrated sound in the back of his throat and that's when Osprey spun. Retger's sword tip came up but Osprey batted it away with the flat of his hand, a growl welling up from his throat.

Despite the growl, his words were incredibly measured. "I swear this to you, House Shrike, I will spill my own blood before spilling hers. I will take any pain she gives without lifting a hand against her. I will cut off my own hands before harming her."

Retger's mouth tightened and he shook his head, looking at me instead of Osprey. "I don't trust him, and I don't really care what he says. You should come with us, Aella. There are five of us – if Wing Ivo is truly on our side – and one of him. This Wing can't stop us if you want to go with us."

I shook my head in denial. I knew perfectly well how fast Osprey was with that blade and how strong Os was. Five of us would hardly slow him. But that wasn't what was stopping me. I had my own plans. And they didn't involve running anymore. If I kept running, I'd be running forever, and then who would save Osprey from himself?

"Go, brother," I said gently. "This task is mine. I mean to see it through."

He surprised me. I'd expected to have to fight him more, but he dropped Zayana's hand and leaned in to give me a brotherly half-hug, eyes never leaving Osprey as if he expected him to strike at a moment's notice.

"Relentless," he said – our family motto – and I echoed it back.

"Relentless."

"I trust you to make this choice, Shrikeling, but if he hurts you we will find him and kill him in the most creative way we can imagine – and between us all, we can imagine quite a lot." He slipped a knife into my belt – never a bad choice of gift – and I smiled in gratitude.

Then he turned back, nodded sharply at Ivo, and said, “We’ll have a fight and a half getting out of here. Let’s take the back way.”

“Is there one?” Ivo asked, his gaze still locked on where Osprey and I stood frozen, unwilling to move before the others were gone.

“There’s always a back way if you know how to look for it,” Retger was saying, and then he turned the corner and they were gone. There was a murmur from the monks nearby.

CHAPTER TWENTY-ONE

I cleared my throat and looked to Osprey. "And now there is you and me."

His eyes lit and he snatched another toothpick from his sleeve, but he didn't stick it between his teeth he just looked at me and looked and looked, his face drinking me up like he'd never expected to see it again and thought the sight might be snatched away at any moment.

Behind him, I saw the monks stepping away from the walls and turning to lift books and valuables from the ruin of the floor.

"If you must take me to your brother, then I will go," I said, catching Osprey's bright blue eyes.

He ignored the statement.

"You must hear this, House Apidae. What you tried to do," he said, rolling the toothpick between two fingers, the slightest hint of a smile on his lips, "was valiant."

"Getting my brother and Zayana to safety?"

He shook his head and his eyes were alight with an emotion I couldn't read.

"Trying to carve out the feather from my chest – at great cost to yourself. It lost you valuable time in fleeing. It's why he managed to catch you again." He swallowed and his face fell. "I tried to get to you. But I was weak, and I couldn't manifest after that stab to my chest. I beat and beat on the door, but I was too weak to save you."

My arms crossed over my belly and my hands grabbed my opposite hips as if to protect me from myself. "What you tried to do was valiant, too."

A furrow appeared in his brow and he tilted his head.

"Stabbing yourself all those times. Doing it to keep from harming me."

His cheeks colored and he looked away. He spoke almost to himself, "It wasn't enough. It's never enough."

"Are you still in a lot of pain?" I tried to keep my voice gentle. "Are the wounds healing?"

He shrugged as if it was nothing, but Os appeared behind him in a flurry of purplish-white light and glowing feathers, he hovered behind Osprey, wrapping one wing around him, the other branching out as if to ward off evil.

"You understood what I was trying to tell you," Osprey said, clearing his throat as if there was something else he wanted to tell me and couldn't. "You figured it out?"

"He's your brother," I said. "Like the two brothers on the coin – the ones who wanted different things and started a war."

Osprey nodded, his piercing blue eyes meeting mine. "I didn't want a war."

"There will be one anyway," I said with a shrug. "And more people will die if we leave it to chance. Like what's going on outside right now."

"That's why I have to rely on other people to set this right." He was so grave as he spoke. It made him look older.

I had so many questions to ask him but all of them felt too personal. I settled for a statement. "You have the same blue eyes as Juste. But the rest is different because your mothers are different. So, your father …"

"House Osprey raised me. And until I was twelve, I thought that General Petren was my father. I consider him that still," he said quietly. "But I am the Emperor's bastard."

I didn't like how he said that word, as if he were judging himself by it.

"Who knows this?" I asked, swallowing.

"Juste does. My father does. The emperor does. Ivo has guessed it. He was my friend when I was newly Hatched."

"And Juste torments you with it."

"What else would Le Majest do with such information?" He winked - one of his terrible, not-funny-at-all winks. I was starting to wonder if they were a nervous tick. "But it's more than that. He's the reason this feather is in my chest. He's the one who tied those children to me - tied their fates to my obedience. A boon he asked of our father - a way to help give him a leg up."

"A leg up in what?" I asked, and his mouth snapped shut. "You can't tell me."

His gaze met mine again, open and pleading but silent.

"But I can guess. The Winged Empire kills off members of a family to make the bloodline stronger. They killed your mother to make you Hatch. And now that I know more, I'm guessing they did it for other reasons."

He nodded, looking away.

"They would normally kill you for Juste, wouldn't they? The previous emperors used to kill their brothers and sisters. Which means you've been left alive for a reason." I paused, thinking. "As a spare in the event that something happens to your dear brother?"

He nodded.

"But you can't do anything to him to harm him and you must wait, obedient and patient for your own death."

He nodded at that.

"Osprey," it was mostly a whisper but partly an aching gasp. His burden was so heavy.

His eyes snapped back to mine. "I've been ordered to hunt you and bring you back, but I'm not going to do it, Aella. I've thought long and hard about it. I've tried to think of ways out of it. So has Ivo. There are so few that might work and all of them have severe consequences, but I've chosen one. It's just … I just need … I wanted to find you first." He paused, licking his lip nervously, and then biting it as if he was trying to catch the words that kept slipping away. When he started again, he was calm and measured. "I wanted to tell you that your betrothal to him is more dangerous than you think, and it has put you in grave peril. Forget the Single Wing for now. Bide your time. You need to run as far and as fast as you can. You must not let him marry you."

"You can't kill him, can you? That isn't your plan." I guessed. He smiled sadly, pleased at my clever guess but his eyes still welling with some new emotion. "And even if you could, you wouldn't. Because you don't just murder people."

"I don't," he agreed. He was so beautiful when he looked at me with those tragic eyes.

"And because of that, you wouldn't condone Ivo or me killing him for you."

He looked down and away, guilt filling his features. He wished he could ask. But I knew he never would.

I gasped as the realization struck me.

"Please don't tell me that you plan to sacrifice yourself. Again."

He still didn't meet my eye. "House Apidae, I can think of only one way to free you. I came only to say goodbye. There is still time to catch up with your brother and go with him." He looked up at me with agonized eyes. "I hope you can forgive me. I wanted this one selfish thing – the chance to say goodbye to you." He swallowed as the floor of the monastery trembled. "It was – perhaps – too much to ask."

"Of all the foolish, ridiculous, noble things." I was shaking my head, my teeth gritted together. Something outside the door boomed and the floor shook. "And here I am talking to you about it when we should be running – both of us."

"Yes, you must run, House Apidae. Fly free," he said, his eyes boring into me. "Forget this plan to go to my brother."

"I will."

He gave me one of his rare smiles, pleased by my answer, and then sank to his knees so suddenly that I barely managed not to stumble backward.

"Have you been hurt?" I couldn't keep the flare of panic out of my voice.

He shook his head, his eyes meeting mine again and a look

of utter vulnerability there. It was as if I was sinking deep within him.

"Take my life, House Apidae. I am bound to hunt you down, but you are not meant to be hunted. You are meant to be free - a symbol to our people. Already, I hear whispers on the streets of a woman with bee manifestations. A woman who will guide freedom to these shores. Free yourself of the Winged Empire. End my life and the hunt that threatens you."

I shook my head, shocked. The bees raging in my head so that I could hardly think.

But the resolution in his eyes didn't fade.

"I understand," he said, drawing one of his daggers from his belt. "It is too much to ask. I will do this myself. Please know," a gentleness came over his face. "Though I have known you but a short time, you have breathed life again into the banked ashes of my heart and given me the courage to do what should have been done years ago. You should go now. You don't need to see this. No one will hunt you when I'm gone."

My voice felt too small, the buzz of my bees so loud that it drowned out all thought. "He'll only send someone else."

He shook his head, his eyes on mine tender. "He chooses to torture that which becomes precious to me. When I am gone, he will forget you. Be free, House Apidae."

He put the dagger to his throat, and I leapt forward and caught his wrist.

"Don't! You're wrong. It won't end with that," I said breathlessly. "Your brother will have me back one way or another. Suicide would end your part in it, certainly, but you are not the only one who obeys his commands. Or haven't you seen the fires consuming the city or the wave of Blue washing over it?"

He swallowed and his bird bobbed a little, flickering in and out as if he couldn't maintain the manifestation.

"I will do anything to save you from him, House Apidae. You must believe me when I tell you that. I will gladly take this blade to my throat. Please, follow your brother and leave this to me."

"I think I have a better idea, Vasyklo," I said gently, and his eyes lit with my use of his name. Tenderness filled me, seeping into my eyes and heart. He'd been willing to give up everything to let me be free. Just like I would give everything to carve out freedom for my family. How could that fail to melt my heart? I reached out and cupped his cheek with one hand and his eyes widened. "But it will take a lot of trust."

"I give you my trust," he said, clearing his throat to push back emotion. "I give you with it my life – what is left of it – my sword, bound though it is – and my honor which is the only thing I can still claim as mine," he said fervently. He sheathed his knife and opened his palms, lifting them out to me. "With these empty palms, my fate is yours. I can hunt you no more, torture you no more. I surrender completely. But you must kill me, Apidae. For I can vow all I want, but my actions are bound to obedience as long as I am alive."

I sank down onto my knees before him and he gasped.

"Not used to that?" I asked, quirking an eyebrow. "That's surprising from the son of an emperor."

"Bastard of an emperor," he corrected with a ghost of a grin. It made his dimple show and my heart stutter.

"May I?" I asked, waiting for his confused nod before I parted his jacket. His breath drew in, but he held still for me, like an injured stallion would hold still as you freed him from a tangle of Forbidding – if he trusted you. His eyes on me were steady and full of faith as I unbuttoned his shirt beneath with care. He reached out to tuck one of my tangled curls behind my ear, tending to me even as I tended to him.

"Make it quick," he whispered, as if he thought I was baring his heart for the dagger.

His chest exposed; I peeled the bandage back from the festering wound there. I gasped at the sight of it. It looked terrible. Rather than glowing, little strings of lightning danced up and down the blackened feather. The part I'd tried to cut out dangled limply, hanging on by a thread to the rest. And around the rest of the feather, the skin was hot and swollen, colored in hues that shouldn't be seen on a healthy body.

"It's a sight to see, isn't it?" Osprey asked grimly.

As gently as possible, I placed my palm against the wound. He hissed.

"This is the part where you need to trust me." I swallowed, worried about my plan. What if it didn't work? What if it made things worse? "Can you do that?"

"I don't think you should cut it out," he said hoarsely. "It didn't seem to work the first time. You need to end this, House Apidae."

"Trust me," I whispered, leaning in and touching my forehead to his as he had once done for me. I put my other hand on the back of his neck, gently cupping it, holding him in this forehead-to-forehead embrace.

"I trust you," he whispered, his breath warm, filling the space between us. He closed his eyes as if waiting for the blade.

I pulled my palm back slowly from his chest and as it retreated, a single glowing bee detached and settled onto his wound - one bright glowing spot on his dark skin.

He gasped at the same moment that the bee wriggled across his wound and then buried itself in the bubbled, open flesh, digging deeper and deeper. He moaned, biting his lip like he was fighting pain. I eased our embrace, giving him space to fight against the pull of pain.

"It's going right to the heart of it all," I assured him. "Just like we do with Forbidding trees. We burn out their hearts."

His eyes snapped open. "You're not going to ..."

"Yes," I said, trying not to make him panic, "it's going to burn the Forbidding right out of your heart. It's going to burn out the ties of that feather and then it will weave you back together and plant honey in the wound of the predator. Won't you, bees?" I smiled down at the one who had answered my request. "You wanted me to be free, Osprey. I want you to be free, too."

"I trust you," he gasped. His face stretched with pain and his hands spasmed, but after a moment of heavy breathing, it seemed to pass and he leaned in close, forehead to mine once more. "I trust you, House Apidae. And I give you my loyalty." He shook his head in wonder. "What sort of girl gives her whole self for others as you do? How could I not be moved when I see that?"

He bent his head, his lips parting gently and my breath fluttered in my chest like a caged butterfly, my lips parting in response to his. I wanted him to kiss me – hoped he might. And just the wanting of it was a fleeting pleasure I wished I could snatch from the air and hold tight to my heart.

"I – " My words were cut off as a vision rocked me in place.

CHAPTER TWENTY-TWO

My sight blurred and then I was seeing something – but not through the eyes of my bees – not really. This was so much stranger than that was. A snake wriggled past my vision – so thick and large that I gasped. For a moment, it blocked everything out. When it slid aside, I was looking at someone from a strange angle.

A woman in a pale silk robe stood before me, her dark hair swept back and a crown of feathers on her head – a Skybinder. One who took the oaths of people and kept community records. Deaths. Births. Marriages. Exchanges of property. They rarely visited Far Reach. I'd only seen one once before, but her serene expression and the way her movements were delicate and bird-like was as familiar as her silk robe and feather crown – all Skybinders looked and moved like that. The only difference was this odd angle. I was looking at her from waist height. And then someone spoke, and it felt as if the sound itself was resonating through me.

"A marriage in absentia, Skybinder, for I am in haste and do not wish to be delayed," the voice alone left a swell of dread bubbling through me.

"But Le Majest," the Skybinder's words stumbled over each other and her serene expression looked close to cracking. "Why the rush? Surely any maiden would be grateful for your attentions and be honored to be part of the ceremony – as is the tradition."

"Surely," the rumbling voice said sarcastically. Juste. And I was watching from the honeycomb in his belly, wasn't I? That's why the snake kept blocking my vision as it wrapped round and round his waist. It was odd that he didn't cover the wound up, unsightly as it was. He was speaking again, this time in a more measured tone. "And yet, I feel the need to issue greater protection for this maiden and dedicate all the might of the Winged Empire to finding her and keeping her safe and at peace. And how can I justify such devotion without the bonds of marriage between us?"

"We have performed such ceremonies in the past," the Skybinder stuttered. "But only in the most dire circumstances. A man who had sailed here, whose betrothed was far away and who wished her to inherit came to me once. He was hours from death. He sought to see her taken care of after he passed. I considered that circumstance dire enough to allow it. But you say your beloved is here on this continent. Can you not wait a few short days for her to be recovered? It is always better for your friends and family to celebrate with you. Perhaps Le Majest would appreciate being here. He would be honored to be included in your great decision."

There was a shift and wobble to my view and then a blade filled my vision and I was so close to the Skybinder that all I saw was her silken robe and the blade pressed against her belly, tip-first.

"Have you ever had your belly sliced open, your insides brought outside and examined?" Juste said in a low voice. "I have. It's an unmaking feeling, like you are no longer human. And when I was woven back together again, there were cords left that bound me in ways I detest. But there will be no one to bind you back together. You'll be discarded here, left to gasp your way into the next life. Unless you understand what is needed of you."

"I don't understand why you need me at all," the Skybinder said, bravely, but with a wavering voice. Her cool façade was gone completely. "If you wish to take the girl, I'm sure you can place a blade to her belly, too. Why do you need me to record it in my books, Le Majest?"

His snort gusted – a combination of humor and derision.

"There are those who respect laws and traditions who will find that this sears them to their very souls." He meant Osprey, of course. "My snake tightens his grip, and soon they will choke on his loops and coils."

Her courage must have failed her. All I heard was a squeak and then her defeated words.

"What name shall I write next to yours, Le Majest?"

"Aella of House Shrike. I'll spell it if writing has also failed you."

I knew it was coming, but still, my breath seized in my chest. It doesn't mean anything, Aella. I leaned into the furious chant of my bees. It doesn't. They raged with me, a tiny protective storm in the middle of my despair. It's just words written on a paper without your permission.

And yet it felt like it meant something.

I heard the scritch of pen on paper and my range of vision changed again as Juste backed up. I could see lines of blue-clad Claws with their white embroidery swirling up sleeves and across wide shoulders. And the worried face of the feather-crowned Skybinder. She finished writing and looked up, chin held high.

"And now you bind us."

Her mouth dropped open.

"That's highly unconventional, Le Majest. In absentia? We only ever do that in person."

"But you don't need her here."

"I don't know the girl!" she protested. "I've never felt her essence. I can't make a bond like that with nothing to work with."

Her face was full of horror.

"I think you can," Juste said in a low voice. "I have a piece of her right here."

Her eyes swiveled downward and she seemed to look right at me.

No, at the honeycomb in Juste's belly.

My vision collapsed and so did I. I shuddered, nausea rolling over me in waves.

It was a moment before I realized that Osprey had caught me. That he was clutching me to his chest with gentle strength. My eyes fluttered open.

"House Apidae." He sounded breathless. His finely sculpted face was inches from mine, eyes wide with worry. "Are you hurt?"

I moaned. And then pain roared through me, blinding me to everything else. I fumbled at my jacket and managed to tear it open and pull down the collar of my tunic. There, so high on my chest, it was almost nipping the collarbone, was the culprit. My skin was red and raised and agonizingly painful and under the skin, shining like the moon, was a silver feather.

Osprey hissed, nearly dropping me in his surprise. My head spun and nausea rippled through me.

"No," I gasped. My bees were so loud they made me shudder

as they ricocheted through my head over and over, furious and violent.

"What happened?" he asked, dread in his voice. His eyes met mine.

"He married me," I choked out. "Against my will. In absentia, they call it."

He gasped as horror and something like devastation washing over his face.

"He bound me to him," I choked out. But he knew that. He'd seen the feather.

My whole body was quivering. Osprey swallowed and I knew exactly what he was thinking – that whatever plans we had to defy the crown prince had just fallen apart because he was bound to obey and now, I was bound, also. I didn't know how or what might happen, but there was magic in my heart, binding me. Magic that I didn't want.

I felt violated. I closed my eyes for a brief moment, unable to hold back the tears spilling from their corners.

Osprey drew me into his warm embrace, and I almost flinched before I remembered it was him. Every touch felt like too much. He tucked my head under his chin and I tried not to let my horror keep me from what comfort I could accept. I tried to let myself sink into his powerful chest, let myself cling to his strength. Just for a minute. Just for one moment. Just long enough to catch my breath.

"I understand," he whispered. "I understand what it's like."

There was jagged pain in his voice as he whispered to me. It reminded me of my plan. It reminded me about why I'd done this.

"Osprey," I whispered, not trusting my voice.

"House Apidae." His voice was so warm it was like hot honey.

"I'm not done what I began. Can you trust me just a little more?"

"My heart is already in your hands," he whispered. "Break it if you must, but I will not take it back now."

The weight of his promise – the utter devotion of it – rocked me and I looked up into his eyes, so wide and trusting.

"Please don't be afraid," I said and then I gently removed his belt.

He watched me with a furrowed brow, his breath hitched like he could hardly believe what I was doing. I paused for just a moment before stripping his scabbards from the belt and carefully wrapping it around his wrists.

"I wish I could do this another way," I said as I cinched it tight and tied it.

He swallowed. "What are you doing?"

I slid his scabbards onto my own belt. I wouldn't lose his short swords. I'd keep them with me.

"Can you hold still a moment?" I asked in a tiny voice and his faint nod told me he would.

I reached into his pocket, my eyes never breaking their hold on his. I pulled out the lace-lined handkerchief I knew would be there and folded it up to a long, narrow fold and then reached up and covered his gorgeous blue eyes with it, tying it gently, but firmly, behind his head. I missed the sight of them already.

"Can you dismiss Os?"

I hadn't realized it, but he'd been hovering over us both protectively. He winked out like a blown-out candle.

I took a deep breath.

"If he has a feather in you, then he can control you," Osprey said grimly. "Though I applaud your effort. Were you planning all along to steal me?"

"You can't go willingly with me – not under your orders, can you?"

"If we left here alive, it would only have been with you as my captive."

"Ah, but it didn't work out that way and now I need to keep you with me while the bees work. I suppose your dear brother didn't think to order you to avoid capture, did he?"

"No." He seemed amused.

"That shows you how little he knows me."

"You're trying to save me again," Osprey said almost fondly. "Even from myself."

"Yes," I agreed, helping him to his feet. The monastery rocked again and there wasn't a monk in sight. "The trick now will be to try to get you out of this city in the middle of a revolution without getting either of us killed."

"House Apidae?"

I paused. "Yes?"

"I still trust you."

"I hope that this is a good idea," I said and slipped one hand under his bicep to guide him carefully through the mess on the floor and toward the door. "Because it's the only one I have."

CHAPTER TWENTY-THREE

If I was grateful for one thing, it was that we were close to the western wall of the city. If I could get free of the monastery and make it to that wall, then maybe I could make my way out of the city and back to the undertrails. It would be difficult to fight my way through the Forbidding with no horse and no supplies and a blindfolded captive, but difficult was not impossible.

I rubbed at the cuff around my wrist. It burned constantly now that Osprey was near, but I didn't want to remove it. I'd grown attached to that cuff and not just for the sense of safety it brought me in helping me know where Osprey was.

"Do you have a plan to escape the city?" Osprey asked as I crept out the door of the monastery.

"My plan is to try to stay hidden, and when I can't, to fight like the Forbidding is clawing at me until I get you out of this place."

He smirked. "It's your kind of plan, House Apidae. I don't suppose you can do me a favor?"

"What kind of a favor?" I breathe, looking in every direction. The street seemed bare except for rubble. Some of the buildings were scorched and others still in flames but the chaos and noise were one street over, leaving us an opportunity to dart across the empty street, so long as they hadn't left someone behind to scout for us. But in this city, you couldn't rely on quiet to mean "safe."

I took the first step out, trying to remember to watch his steps as well as mine.

My chest burned as I walked and with it, my fury rose. Juste Montpetit took everything from me. My father, my family, my home, and now my freedom. And he was going to get away with it unless I could stop him.

I ground my teeth at the thought.

"I'd love one of my toothpicks," Osprey said. "They're in a tiny pocket in my sleeve."

I couldn't help the soft laugh that escaped me. "We're sneaking through a city in chaos and I have you bound and blindfolded, and you want a toothpick?"

We'd made it halfway across the street, but the noise was growing louder, and I was getting nervous.

"I'll get you one when we reach the alley," I said. "I have a question for you, too."

"Let it loose."

He seemed almost at ease, following me. It didn't make any sense at all. When he was his own man, he was tortured and distraught, but as a prisoner, he seemed almost lighthearted.

"If you are truly brothers, does that mean that if he dies then you'll inherit the crown?"

"Just married and already dreaming of the life of a widow?" he teased, but I could hear the pain in his tone. I waited, concentrating on picking our way across the street. This was nearly impossible with the care I had to take for him. I needed a horse or some other way to carry him.

After a moment, he went on. "I don't want the crown. And the game is rigged so that I'll certainly never wear it. But yes – if he dies, I am the last of the blood of House Swan."

"You didn't manifest a swan," I said. We'd reached the alley on the other side and I paused there, letting us catch our breath and casting worried glances in every direction. The alley appeared empty – but a lot of things appeared other than they really were.

"I didn't," he said, seeming amused at my comment.

I reached for his sleeve and found the tiny pocket, slipping a toothpick out of it and bringing it to his lips. They were surprisingly soft as he accepted the toothpick from my fingers and for just a moment, I wondered what it would be like to kiss him. I leaned in close, imagining it, emboldened by his blindfold. But what would he think of me if I kissed him when I'd just been married to his brother? Something in my heart lurched at the thought and I drew back again. Besides, it wasn't right to take advantage of him when he was my captive.

"Do it," he whispered, his breath so close I could feel it.

"Do what?" I asked, my heart beating so fast I couldn't seem to catch my breath.

He only smirked in response and it was all I could do not to snatch that toothpick and kiss him. That would show him and his smirks!

"Let's move," I whispered, drawing him down the alley. He followed me with easy grace, despite his captivity.

I steered him carefully around the obstacles in the alley – items people had dropped while fleeing violence, objects that might have been carried as weapons, spatters of blood and other fluids that I didn't want to identify. My arm wrapped around him as we fled. He needed more guidance than I would have expected with his hands bound and his eyes covered and that required more touch. But there was something about wrapping my arm around his warm body that made me feel vulnerable – even more vulnerable than the screams and cries in the street did. It was fully dark now, and the fires in the distance blazed, casting the city into a haze of flickering orange light.

Maybe they were trying to burn out the evil here, just like we tried to burn it out of the Forbidding. I suspected it was not the evil who were suffering tonight. The thought made my heart hurt. This was all wrong – all of it. And someone should have led these people to a better way before they exploded like this.

Osprey stumbled. I'd failed to notice a broken sign in his path.

"I'm sorry," I gasped. "I'm so sorry for all of this."

"I'm not sorry that you're trying to save me."

The outer city wall was before us now, and I sighed in relief. I just had to follow it to a gate. Once we were outside the city, I could ease up on our pace.

I followed the stone wall, nervous as the sounds and cries grew louder with every step we took. We were approaching a bright flare ahead.

"Are we almost at the gate?" Osprey whispered. He was chewing his toothpick nervously.

"I think it's close," I replied, peering down the quiet street to the source of the noise and light. There wouldn't be a way to avoid people if I wanted to get out.

"The gates will be closed. It's standard protocol for an uprising," Osprey said calmly. "I'd offer Os to fly over the wall, but we both know that if I get up on him, my orders will force me to take you back to Le Majest. I won't have a choice. So, you'll have to do this without my help. The Claws have a codeword. It will get you out, but if you use it, it will be reported to Le Majest and if he ever finds you, he will certainly punish you."

"As if marrying him is not punishment enough."

He snorted a laugh. "If you use it, it tells them that you're considered an exception to their orders. It can get you through the gate. It's a phrase. You tell the Claws, 'this trap has a beating heart.' Can you remember that?"

"Easily. Juste certainly likes creepy comments. But there's a flaw in your thinking. They're going to notice that you're my prisoner."

"Yes," he agreed, a grimace on his face as he hunched over his chest. The bee must be at work. It's power was in healing magic. And while it would help, it likely hurt, too.

"Then it's not much of a plan."

"Unless you go without me," he gasped. "And you should. I'm only going to slow you down. If you leave me tied up in the cellar of one of these buildings, it will be days before they find me. It will give you a head start."

I huffed. "No. I'm not leaving you behind, Osprey. You're as much a prisoner of the crown prince as I am. You're as pursued and trapped and tied as me, and I won't leave you to your fate."

"Just promise that you'll leave me if I become a liability." He sounded desperate.

"No!" The thought of it made something ache inside.

"Aella."

My heart froze in my chest. He never said my actual name. On his tongue, it sounded like a caress. I held my breath until he spoke again.

"Can you do one more thing for me? One last request."

"Anything," I gasped, leaning in close.

"I can hear that we're getting close to the action. When we get there, we might not survive what comes next. There's little I can do to thank you for what you've done for me."

"I've done nothing but complicate your life."

"And I don't have the right to ask – and yet, I think I will." He turned his head and spat his toothpick out. His next words were rough, almost harsh. "Come closer."

My heart sped as I moved from beside him to stand in front of him.

"Closer, still."

I stepped closer again, so that I could have embraced him.

"Just once." It sounded like a plea. "Just once before I die, grant me this one gift." He paused, and I watched his dark throat bob as he swallowed down whatever was making him nervous. "Let me taste your lips. Burn yourself across my memory one last time."

I froze. Had he really said that? I could feel the heat rushing up to my cheeks.

"I … not me." I stumbled over my words, my tongue felt too thick to speak. The idea of him still offering this rattled me. Didn't he see me as tainted by my marriage to his brother? Even if it was against my will, I felt that way. "You deserve better. You should choose better."

"I choose you."

"I'm hurting you. I'm wrecking you. With every choice that I make. Even the ones made for me," I said, feeling oddly vulnerable in this moment.

"I still want you," he said, his certainty fading as he tagged on another thought. "Unless you don't want me."

He leaned forward, slowly, his tied hands finding one of mine, his forehead slowly coming to rest against mine.

"It's okay that you don't, House Apidae," he said huskily. "It's your choice to make, too."

My heart was so loud that I couldn't even hear the fighting in the distance. I tried to take a breath, but it was a faint, unstable thing.

Before he could say more, I caught his face between my hands and pulled his mouth down. And then his lips had found mine and he kissed me so gently, it was like a hummingbird kissing a flower. I gasped and one of his sweet lips slipped between mine and I couldn't think. It felt … like blasphemy … for me to kiss him. I wasn't worthy of it. I didn't have the right. And yet I didn't want it to ever stop.

My hands reached up to tangle through his short hair and my breath came back gusting in startled bursts. He made a pleased sound into my lips and then kissed me again, deeper, more roughly as if he could show me with just his kiss everything he'd do if his hands weren't tied and his eyes not bound with that handkerchief. His tongue found mine and my thoughts swirled and tangled like they were part of the Forbidding. I couldn't catch them, couldn't keep them in place, could only add my own passion and desperate longing to his until one was so bound up in the other that they were one shared hope.

And it hurt, hurt, hurt because I knew it couldn't last, that we were stealing something we couldn't own, asking for something the skies would never give. And I didn't care that it hurt. I wanted to keep hurting like this forever.

I kissed him like I hoped it would and felt the urgent roughness of his kiss responding to it.

I hadn't realized that I'd manifested my bees until I opened my eyes to their golden glow. The corners of Osprey's lips curled up and his dimple flashed in his cheek.

"You're the sweetness of honey and the sharpness of the sting all rolled into one, House Apidae."

Oh, sweet skies they'd really stung him! I could see the mark on his lip where it was swelling up.

"I'm so sorry," I gasped, putting my hand over my own swollen lips.

"I'm not."

He kissed me again, stung lip and all, taking his time as if he could make one kiss last a thousand year. Then he rested his forehead against mine.

"Just like honey." He sighed. "If I had to bet on anyone getting what they wanted, I'd bet on you, House Apidae, but even if your plan fails and I perish, I'll never be sorry that we stole these kisses."

"I don't want to lose you," I gasped, startled by the confession.

"I don't think you can," he whispered, his breath rough and

lips still parted.

I would have kissed him again, but the sound of marching and a harsh order caught my attention. I froze, listening. They were on the other end of the street from the glowing gate, marching this way.

"We need to go, now!" I said, urgently wrapping my arm around him and pushing him forward. My bees vanished immediately except for one that spun round and round my head. I cursed and it finally left me.

The moment that it did, I realized that something was wrong. Osprey stumbled, his head lolling to one side.

"Osprey?" I hissed, still trying to pull him along.

Pain flared through my chest so suddenly that I stumbled from the agony of it. With the pain came a pull, drawing me back toward the center of the city.

Chapter Twenty-Four

"Keep trying you Forbidding-taken dust-kisser!" I snarled. I'd had no idea the feather could do that, but I knew I didn't dare follow its pull. My new husband only wanted one thing for me – torture. And what he wanted for the precious boy who'd just kissed me was death. He could go kiss dust.

There was a shout from down the street toward the gate and a dark mass of silhouettes stepped into the street between me and the gate.

"Down there! I hear them marching!" I heard a rough voice cry.

"Back, you Imperial fools! Back, or we'll spray you with fire and soak you in death. This land is ours and we'll live free or die to make it so!"

There was a roar of agreement around the voice and I agreed with the sentiment, too, but now I was stuck between a crowd of rebels and the marching feet of Claws. On the Claw side, I heard the answering order sound.

"Prepare arms! Ready the line!"

The sound of boots shuffling told me it was being obeyed.

I cursed, looking for a way out. The alley we'd used to come to this street was past the line of Claws and I didn't see any other alleys. There were doors lining the street on both sides – doors of darkened homes. Should I try one of them?

"Osprey?" I whispered. All his weight was leaning on me.

He moaned unintelligibly. I shot a glance at him and saw the golden feather flaring in his breast. My breath quickened. The bee was doing its job – and the timing couldn't be worse. He would need me to protect him while he went through this. He couldn't fend for himself like this, not even if I hadn't trussed him up like a goat.

I turned back to the task at hand, my belly flipping nervously. I wasn't sure if I could make it as far as the closest door. And what if it didn't open when I made it there?

But we were stuck between two opposing forces. What other option was there?

I struggled toward the door with Osprey moaning in my arms. He was conscious enough to move his feet – which I was grateful for. I wouldn't be able to carry him – but he was harder to move with his hands tied. Frustrated, I tugged at the belt, untying it and slinging it around him, cinching it around both of us so that I'd have at least that advantage in trying to keep him close. After a moment, I tugged off the blindfold, too. He didn't need it right now and it looked suspicious. His eyes were shut, mouth hanging open.

I cursed. But at least it was less obvious this way that he was my prisoner.

It took all my strength to half-drag him to the nearest door. I tugged on the handle, cursing wildly when it was locked, just as I'd feared.

My palms were sweating, body aching from exertion, chest screaming to me to follow the pull. I gritted my teeth and tried to think.

The Claws were so close that I could see the embroidery on their coats, bright in the dancing light that swathed the city. Smoke and ash swirled in the air around them and around the dark shadows coming from the other direction. I was stuck. Trapped. I could cry out to tell them to stop … but then what? None of them would listen. I needed a plan and I was coming up with nothing.

Panicked, I wrapped my arms around Osprey as his head fell to my shoulder. I had to think. I had to get him out of here.

Something glowing and bright – a bottle, I thought – soared through the air, striking the ground where we'd been standing just moments ago. A crash sounded and then fire flared, rushing across the pool of fluid where the bottle had crashed. It shot up in a blazing wall between the Claws and the revolutionaries, lighting the entire street in a single flash.

Everyone was closer than I'd realized, their faces bright in the light of the flash – hundreds of Claws on one side and dozens of rebels on the other. Their eyes all swiveled to me and I had to clamp my jaw tight to keep from squeaking in sudden fear.

The light from the flames danced along sword blades on either side. And I didn't know which of them to turn to. On the one hand, the rebels shared my ideals, but the way they were sacking the city wasn't what I wanted and they weren't going to win. On the other hand, the Claws would likely let me live if I told them who I was, only to drag me to Juste as his reluctant bride.

We all stood frozen for one heartbeat.

"That's Wing Osprey," the Claw officer said in shock, pointing at Osprey in my arms. He was a hulking man whose Claw coat barely stretched over thick muscles. "What have you done to him, girl?"

At the same time, one of the rebels spoke. She was a woman in her mid-forties and the cleaver in her hand was already streaked with gore.

"Choose wisely, girl. You're either with them or with us. If you're with us, slit the throat of that Wing and step over to this side."

"And if I'm not with you?" I shot back.

"Then we'll hack you down." Her voice was ice cold. "With no mercy."

"Then you're no better than the Empire of War and Wings."

"Justice is worth the price of a few soft girls who can't choose a side," she snarled.

"Touch the Wing and it will be the last thing you do," the Claw officer said, as if he was just waiting for his chance to speak.

I gripped Osprey with both hands, my heart aching with frustration. These rebels should be more than this. The rebellion should be more than just ousting one enemy to make way for a worse regime. It should be about protecting the weak, about restoring justice and freedom.

Frustration filled me and with it, my bees began to rise within me. I had something to say before I blew my plan to pieces with all this pent-up rage.

"I'd hoped to side with you," I told the rebels, "But here you are threatening people you don't even know."

"What do you know, you Imperial dog?"

"I know that there has to be a better way and I know that I'll find it, even if I have to wade through the bile of fools to seize wisdom."

"Is that a no?" she said, tilting her head to the side. "Are you saying that you aren't on our side?"

She took a step forward, the flames still dancing between her and the Claws, but leaving a clear path to me. The Claw closest to me nodded sharply at a gesture from his officer, and took a step closer, too.

"Are you saying that you aren't with us?" he challenged me.

The buzzing was so powerful that I barely heard him. It filled every part of me, making the skin in my fingers and face tingle with the bees need to be released.

"I'm not with any of you," I said boldly, "but very soon, you'll have to decide if you're on my side. A war is coming – a bigger one than this small skirmish – and anyone who loves freedom will have to stand up and defend it."

"Who are you to make such bold claims?" The woman facing me took another step, matched by the Claw on the other side of the flames. She was eyeing him the same way he was eyeing her – both assessing whether it was better to grab me or their clear opponent. She tossed her cleaver to her other hand – a clear threat. One more step and her reach would be enough to slash my throat with that thing – or worse, Osprey's. I didn't dare give her the opportunity.

I relaxed and let go of the hold I had on my bees. They rushed from my hands in a glowing cloud, racing to spread through the crowd on either side of the flames while others spiraled around me like a living shield of insects. Their buzz was so loud I could hardly hear my own voice as I shouted.

BEHIND THE SCENES:

USA Today bestselling author, Sarah K. L. Wilson loves spinning a yarn and if it paints a magical new world, twists something old into something reborn, or makes your heart pound with excitement ... all the better. Sarah hails from the rocky Canadian Shield in Northern Ontario – learning patience and tenacity from the long months of icy cold – where she lives with her husband and two small boys. You might find her building fires in her woodstove and wishing she had a dragon handy to light them for her

Sarah would like to thank Barbara, Melissa and Eugenia for their incredible work in beta reading and proofreading this book. Without their big hearts and passion for stories, this book would not be the same.

Sarah has the deepest regard for the talent of her phenomenal artist Luciano Fleitas who created the gorgeous cover art that accompanies this book. Without his work, it would be so much harder to show off this story the way it deserves. She also wants to thank her editor, Melissa, who tried her best to make this book better. Any errors remaining are all Sarah's.

Thanks also to the Noble Order of Female Fantasy Authors who keep me sane – sort of. And for my beloved husband, Cale and sons Neville and Leif who are endlessly patient as I talk to them about bookish passions.

Visit my website for more information:

www.sarahklwilson.com

www.ingramcontent.com/pod-product-compliance
Lightning Source LLC
Chambersburg PA
CBHW070538310726
48982CB00010B/1402/J

* 9 7 8 1 7 7 7 2 6 4 5 2 9 *